# The
# CODE BUSTERS
## CLUB

CASE #2:

The Haunted
Lighthouse

# Penny Warner

EGMONT
USA
New York

# EGMONT

*We bring stories to life*

First published by Egmont USA, 2012
443 Park Avenue South, Suite 806
New York, New York 10016

1 3 5 7 9 8 6 4 2

www.egmontusa.com
www.pennywarner.com
www.CodeBustersClub.com

LIBRARY OF CONGRESS
CATALOGING-IN-PUBLICATION DATA
Warner, Penny.
The haunted lighthouse / Penny Warner.
p. cm. — (The Code Busters Club ; case #2)
Summary: An enigmatic message leads the Code Busters on a treasure
hunt on creepy Alcatraz Island, where they must use their problem-
solving skills to unravel the mystery.
ISBN 978-1-60684-163-1 (hardback) — ISBN 978-1-60684-362-8 (e-book)
[1. Cryptography—Fiction. 2. Ciphers—Fiction. 3. Alcatraz Island
(Calif.)—Fiction. 4. Mystery and detective stories.] I. Title.
PZ7.W2458Hau 2012
[Fic]—dc23
2012003787

Printed in the United States of America

*To all the Code Busters Club Members,*
*especially Bradley, Luke, Stephanie, and Lyla.*
*And special thanks to Connor Brien!*

# READER

To see keys and solutions to the
puzzles inside, go to the Code Buster's
Key Book & Solutions on page 183.

To see complete Code Busters Club
Rules and Dossiers, and solve
more puzzles and mysteries, go to
**www.CodeBustersClub.com**

# CODE BUSTERS CLUB RULES

## Motto
To solve puzzles, codes, and mysteries and
keep the Code Busters Club secret!

## Secret Sign
Interlocking index fingers
(American Sign Language sign for "friend")

## Secret Password
Day of the week, said backward

## Secret Meeting Place
Code Busters Club Clubhouse

# Code Busters Club Dossiers

## IDENTITY: Quinn Kee

**Code Name:** "Lock&Key"

**Description**
Hair: Black, spiky
Eyes: Brown
Other: Sunglasses

**Special Skill:** Video games, Computers, Guitar

**Message Center:** Doghouse

**Career Plan:** CIA cryptographer
or Game designer

**Code Specialties:** Military code,
Computer codes

## IDENTITY: MariaElena—M.E.—Esperanto

**Code Name:** "Em-me"

**Description**
Hair: Long, brown
Eyes: Brown
Other: Fab clothes

**Special Skill:** Handwriting analysis, Fashionista

**Message Center:** Flower box

**Career Plan:** FBI handwriting analyst or Veterinarian

**Code Specialties:** Spanish, I.M., Text messaging

## IDENTITY: Luke LaVeau

**Code Name:** "Kuel-Dude"

**Description**
Hair: Black, curly
Eyes: Dark brown
Other: Saints cap

**Special Skill:** Extreme sports, Skateboard, Crosswords

**Message Center:** Under step

**Career Plan:** Pro skater, Stuntman, Race car driver

**Code Specialties:** Word puzzles, Skater slang

## IDENTITY: Dakota—Cody—Jones

**Code Name:** "CodeRed"

**Description**
Hair: Red, curly
Eyes: Green
Other: Freckles

**Special Skill:** Languages, Reading faces and body language

**Message Center:** Tree knothole

**Career Plan:** Interpreter for UN or deaf people

**Code Specialties:** Sign language, Braille, Morse code, Police codes

# CONTENTS*

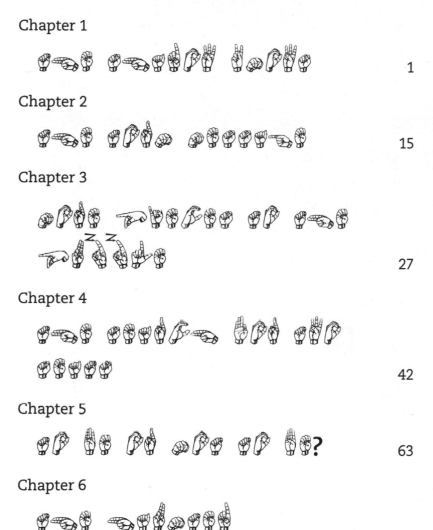

*To crack the chapter title code, check out the CODE BUSTER'S Key Book & Solutions on pages 184 and 194.*

# Chapter 1

"G" uys . . . look at this!" Cody Jones said to her fellow Code Buster Club members, who were spread out in her upstairs bedroom doing homework.

Quinn Kee, the self-appointed leader of the club and math whiz, lay on the floor composing a sudoku puzzle for the others to solve. His ever-present aviator sunglasses rested on top of his spiky black hair.

| | 7 | | | 6 | | | 2 | |
|---|---|---|---|---|---|---|---|---|
| | | 3 | 2 | 9 | 7 | 5 | | |
| | | 6 | 5 | | 4 | 3 | | |
| | 6 | 8 | | | | 7 | 1 | |
| 1 | | 7 | | | | 9 | | 5 |
| | 9 | 5 | | | | 2 | 8 | |
| | | 4 | 8 | | 2 | 1 | | |
| | | 1 | 3 | 5 | 6 | 4 | | |
| | 5 | | | 1 | | | 3 | |

*Code Buster's Solution found on p. 189.*

Luke LaVeau lay sprawled across the bed on his stomach, studying his spelling words. MariaElena Esperanto—M.E. for short—took up her usual spot in Cody's red beanbag chair, writing a poem. Sitting at her desk, Cody pointed to her computer screen. The cryptic message she'd just received had caused the back of her neck to tingle.

To: CodeRed@CodeBustersClub.com

From: TheShadow@Question.com

Subject: Treasure Hunt

Message:

**In darkness yon,**

A shro**uded** night **covers is**land mists.

**Those ha**llowed, **sunken, tired** souls,

**Lively ghosts hope** you'll **see** . . .

A**lone a local treasure.**

**−Z**


Luke and Quinn sat up to see the computer screen. M.E. rolled over to view it. Cody read the message aloud and then turned to them. "Did one of you guys write this?" she asked, raising a suspicious eyebrow. The Code Busters were known for writing and sending coded messages to each other. That's why they'd formed their club. They had recently solved a real crime involving Cody's former neighbor, Mr. Skelton—the man they used to call "Skeleton Man."

"I didn't," M.E. said, her dark eyes wide. She glanced at the two boys.

"Me, either," Luke added, leaning back, his tall, lanky body melting into the comforter.

"Don't look at me!" Quinn said, when Cody turned her attention to him. He scrunched up his face and studied the message again.

"You're *sure* none of you wrote this?" Cody stared at each one of her friends, her red-haired ponytail swishing behind her as she moved her head.

"Uh-uh," Luke said.

"No way." M.E. shook her head.

"Quinn?" Cody asked again when he didn't respond.

"No, I'm telling you! I didn't write it or send it," Quinn said, standing up to get a closer look. "Read it out loud again."

Cody turned back to the screen and read the message once more.

4

*"In darkness yon,*

*A shrouded night covers island mists.*

*Those hallowed, sunken, tired souls,*

*Lively ghosts hope you'll see . . .*

*Alone a local treasure.*

*Z"*

"Sounds like a poem," M.E. said. She was somewhat of a poet herself, always making up riddles in rhyme. She'd memorized "The Raven" by Edgar Allan Poe—and loved reciting it when they had sleepovers, hoping to scare Cody, but she always ended up just scaring herself.

"Dude, if it's a poem, it doesn't make a lot of sense," Luke said, putting aside his study sheet. Cody glanced at his homework and saw a list of unfamiliar words:

*ushoe*

*holocs*

*knomey*

*grande*

*grifen*

*grooft*

*pliglens*

*macres*

*Code Buster's Solution found on p. 189.*

Even though the list looked as if it was written in a foreign language, she knew they were anagrams. Luke's grandmother always made a game of his spelling words by scrambling them up. Luke had to unscramble the letters, which helped him remember how to spell the word correctly.

Luke saw Cody checking out the list and said, "I'm stuck on the last one."

It took her only seconds to figure it out, but instead of blurting out the answer, she gave him a hint. "Try starting with the last letter and ending with the first letter."

"Got it!" he said. "Thanks!"

"Great, now can we get back to this weird message on my computer?"

She read it aloud again. *"A shrouded night covers island mists . . . Lively ghosts hope you'll see . . . Alone a local treasure."*

"So who's this Z dude—the Shadow, or whatever he calls himself?" Luke asked.

"I don't know, but it sounds old-fashioned," M.E. said, wiggling her knee-sock-covered feet. Today her socks had Hello Kitty designs that in no way matched her tie-dyed shirt and denim skirt. Who knew what she'd be wearing tomorrow. "Cody and I are studying poetry in class. That was the way they spoke back in the day."

"We are, too, but not gibberish," Luke argued.

Quinn laughed. "My dad thinks I speak gibberish. Half the time he doesn't know what I'm saying when I speak pig Latin."

M.E. nodded. "Y-may arents-pay o-day, oo-tay!" she said.

*Code Buster's Key and Solution found on pp. 184, 189.*

"I have a feeling we're missing the point here," Cody said.

The others looked at her, waiting for an explanation.

"I think it's a code. After all, someone sent it to us at CodeBustersClub.com, so they obviously know we're into deciphering codes and puzzles."

"So let's decipher it," Quinn said. "M.E., you're good at poetry. What does, '*In darkness yon, / A shrouded night covers island mists*,' mean?"

M.E. frowned. "Uh . . . there's an island in the dark or the fog?"

Quinn nodded, then continued. "What about, '*Those hallowed, sunken, tired souls, / Lively ghosts hope you'll see*' . . . ?"

"I don't know," M.E. said, shrugging. "I'm not an expert."

"Sounds like dead people," Cody offered. "Souls, ghosts . . ."

"And a treasure," Luke added, noting the last line, *"Alone a local treasure."*

"Maybe," Cody said. "But what about those letters in bold?"

"Yeah," Quinn said, leaning toward the screen. "What's up with that?"

"Let me try something." Cody highlighted the message and copied it to a new document. She deleted all the letters that weren't in bold. When she was done, she tried to read the message aloud, but it came out in one long word:

"IdareyoutovisitThehauntedLighthouseonalcatraZ."

She tried again, reading it more slowly.

*Code Buster's Solution found on p. 189.*

"Alcatraz?" Luke asked, with a hint of his Louisiana accent. "That's weird. Our class is going there tomorrow on a field trip."

"We all are," Cody said. All four Code Busters were in the sixth grade, but the girls were in a different class from the boys. The whole sixth grade was heading for the prison island the next day on a class trip.

Cody stared at the translated message and was caught by the words *haunted lighthouse*. She knew there was a lighthouse on Alcatraz. Her teacher, Ms. Stadelhofer, had spent a class on the island once known as "the Rock," which had held many notorious prisoners but was now one of the most popular attractions in the Bay Area. She'd never been there, but she'd heard many stories about the prison, including that it was haunted by prisoners who had died there. Although she didn't believe in ghosts, Cody shivered at the thought. If there was such a thing as spirits returning to haunt a scary place, Alcatraz, with its violent history, would be perfect. But she was sure these were legends, told to attract more tourists to "the Rock."

So who had sent them an e-mail about the lighthouse being haunted? What was behind this mysterious message? And who was Z, aka The Shadow?

"I say we keep an eye out tomorrow for this mysterious 'Shadow' and see what's up."

"I agree!" M.E. said. "This is going to be fun! I can't wait for tomorrow. Maybe we'll see the ghost of Al Capone."

"Who's Al Capone?" Luke asked.

"He was a big gangster in Chicago," M.E. said. "They called him Scarface. He was a bootlegger back when there was Prohibition."

"What's a bootlegger?" Luke asked.

"Someone who sold alcohol when it was illegal," M.E. answered.

Cody's younger sister, Tana, who was deaf, appeared at the door and finger-spelled to Cody:

*[sign language symbols]*

Cody nodded at her sister.

"What did she say?" Luke asked, watching Tana.

Cody showed her friends the signs.

*Code Buster's Key and Solution found on pp. 184, 189.*

The kids copied each of the signs with her.

"Thanks, Tana," Cody said, and finger-spelled that to her sister. *[sign language symbols]*

Cody turned to her friends. "Well, I'll see you guys tomorrow." Quinn packed up his IRONMAN backpack. M.E. gathered her things into her I'M A PRINCESS backpack. Luke stuffed his spelling words into his sports bag and picked up his skateboard before pushing himself up from the bed. They followed Cody down the stairs and said a polite good night to her mother. Cody knew her friends were a little intimidated by her mom, who happened to be a Berkeley police officer. But they also knew Mrs. Jones would be there for them if they ever needed her. She had recently helped them solve the mystery involving Mr. Skelton.

After the others left, Cody kissed her mother good night and took Tana back upstairs to sign her a bedtime story. When she was finished tucking her sister in, Cody returned to her bedroom, pulled out her collection of lighthouse postcards, and crawled under her heart-covered comforter. She flipped through them and sighed contentedly. She'd been collecting the postcards since she'd seen her first one, when she'd lived in the California Gold Country. She'd been attracted to lighthouses because they seemed to symbolize strength and hope during rough times. And she'd been through some rough times, what with her parents getting a divorce, their moving to a new city, and her having to make new friends.

Cody returned the album of postcards to the spot under her bed and turned off the light. But the semidarkness did nothing to help her get to sleep. She stared at the shaft of moonlight on her ceiling, wide awake, puzzling over the cryptic message that had mysteriously appeared in her e-mail box.

When she finally fell asleep, she dreamed about a ghost wearing prison-striped pajamas, flying in and out of a lonely, abandoned lighthouse.

# Chapter 2

"orning, sweetheart," Mrs. Jones said as Cody
entered the kitchen, dressed for school. Winter weather had come early to Berkeley and the rest of the San Francisco Bay Area, stripping the trees of their colorful leaves and laying early morning frost on the lawns and rooftops. Cody had dressed in layers, because her teacher had warned her class that Alcatraz Island would be cold and windy. Cody

had never been to "the Rock," so she made sure she was prepared, wearing her warmest jeans, two long-sleeved T-shirts, Ugg boots, her red hoodie, and a black muffler.

"Ready to go to prison?" Mrs. Jones asked, pouring some orange juice for Cody and Tana.

"You mean school?" Cody asked, grinning at her mom's play on words. "They're the same thing, right?"

Mrs. Jones shook her head at her daughter's joke. "Very funny. You love school, and you know it."

"I don't *love* it," Cody tried to argue. "I just don't hate it."

"That's because you're good at so many subjects. You inherited your brains from me, of course." Mrs. Jones handed Cody a bag lunch and some money to buy souvenirs and to use in case of an emergency.

"I thought I got my *looks* from you," Cody said,

stuffing the lunch and the money into her back-pack.

"Oh, no, you can thank your dad for your adorable freckles and red hair."

Even though her mother and father were divorced, they still got along, which was a relief. They'd just gone their separate ways, for reasons Cody didn't fully understand. Her dad was an attorney—a public defender—and before the split, her parents had often argued about criminal justice matters. She figured that was probably the reason they no longer lived together. But her dad was almost as involved in Tana's and her lives as her mother. Yet Cody didn't enjoy spending every other weekend with her dad. Not that she didn't love her time with him—they always did something fun, like go to the zoo, eat weird foods, or check out the animal skeletons at the University of California campus lab. But it was hard leaving her main home, her cozy bedroom, and her neighborhood friends for her dad's across-town condo.

Cody drank her juice and grabbed the bagel that was waiting for her, then headed for the front door with her backpack.

"Have fun on the Rock!" Mrs. Jones called. "And be good. I don't want you to end up in solitary confinement."

"Don't worry, Mom," Cody called back from the front door. "I'll escape. I've got a nail file and a compass in my backpack. I should be home by Christmas."

"Don't forget your wet suit. It's a mile-and-a-half-long swim from Alcatraz to San Francisco in fifty-degree water."

"I'll add an inflatable—!" She was cut off by Tana's running up and hugging her good-bye.

"I love you," she signed.

"Me, too," Cody signed back.

Cody closed the door behind her, still smiling at her mother's good-bye. As a cop, Mrs. Jones was often serious and strict, but she loved to play games with Cody, especially word games like Banana-grams, Scrabble, and Wacky Words. Every day she'd find a word game that her mother had left in her lunch bag. She peeked in the bag and pulled out today's puzzle—a Wacky Word. Inside a box was a rebus-type puzzle. Cody had to figure out how the words related to the box to figure out the answer.

| L | O | C | K | E | D |
|---|---|---|---|---|---|
|   | ■ |   |   |   |   |
|   |   |   |   |   |   |

*Code Buster's Solution found on p. 190.*

19

Cody figured it out quickly, smiling at how the puzzle related to her field trip, then tucked it back in her lunch bag to share with the other Code Busters.

As was her habit, Cody stopped by the ash tree in her front yard to check the secret compartment—a hidden knothole the size of her fist. Each of the Code Busters had a secret hiding place where they could receive coded messages from one another. M.E.'s was in her flower box. Quinn's was in his doghouse. And Luke found his messages under the front porch of the house where he lived with his *grand-mère*.

Today the knothole was empty. Cody felt a little disappointment that there wasn't a secret note for her, but since they were all going on a field trip, she wasn't surprised.

"Cody!" her mother called from the porch. "Did you drop this?" Her mother held up a scrap of paper. "I found it on the mat."

Cody ran back and took the paper from her mom.

She unfolded it, revealing a message inside. She noticed the note had been torn—the right side and the bottom side had ragged edges. She looked over the letters on the remaining piece of paper, typed in a bold font.

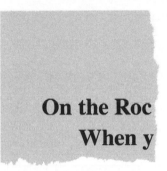

**On the Roc**
**When y**

"Is that another one of your Code Buster secret messages?" her mother asked.

"I guess so," Cody said, although the Code Busters had never left notes on the porch before. She glanced around to see if she could spot any of her friends lurking nearby.

Maybe the note was from Matt the Brat. He was always snooping around the Code Busters, spying on them and trying to intercept their messages.

Maybe he had even sent the strange e-mail that Cody had received last night. He was always up to something.

She looked at the message again. Was this some kind of code? It sure looked like it. But why write a message, tear it up, and leave it on the porch? It made no sense.

"Cody!"

M.E. was walking toward her, wearing another one of her arty outfits. Today she had on bell-bottom jeans covered with purple-and-blue embroidered flowers, and a pink top with a rhine-stone heart on the front. Purple striped socks and red Converse shoes covered her feet, the shoe-laces crisscrossed backward so they tied at the toe. In spite of the winter chill, she'd wrapped her denim jacket around her waist instead of putting it on.

"Did you get a message, too?" M.E. asked when she reached Cody's front yard.

Cody looked at her friend. "You got one?"

"Yeah, I found it on my front porch this morn-ing. It was ripped in half. I couldn't really read it." M.E. dug the note out of her jeans pocket and showed it to her.

Cody took the note and tried to read it out loud, but like her own message, it didn't make any sense. And it had been torn at the top and right-hand side. It said:

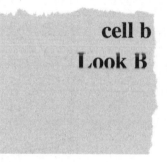

**cell b**
**Look B**

"What's it supposed to mean?" Cody asked.

"I was hoping you'd know," M.E. said, her face crestfallen with disappointment. "Isn't it the same as yours?"

Cody shook her head. She held up her note to

M.E.'s message to compare.

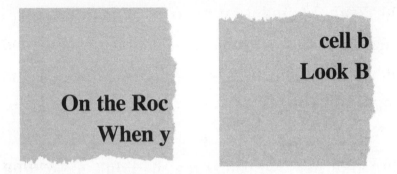

"It *still* doesn't make any sense," M.E. said. "Look, yours is torn, too."

Cody examined the two torn sides of both notes and tried to match the torn bottom of her note to the torn top of M.E.'s.

Bingo. A match.

"They obviously came from the same sheet of paper. See, they've been torn in half right here." She pointed to the ragged right sides of both notes. "And whoever wrote it used the same font. But I still can't make out the message."

Cody and M.E. looked at each other.

"The boys!" Cody said.

"They probably have the other pieces of the message!" M.E. added.

"I'll bet this is Quinn's doing. He loves leaving messages for us to solve. He probably—"

"Dakota Jones!" Cody's mother's voice cut her off.

Cody spun around to see her mother standing at the doorway, one hand holding Tana's hand, the other on her hip. "You're going to be late for school! Get going!"

In all the excitement of finding the message, Cody had lost track of the time. "Sorry, Mom!" she said. She waved 'bye to Tana and finger-spelled,

*Code Buster's Key and Solution found on pp. 184, 190.*

Then Cody hurried down the street toward Berkeley Cooperative Middle School. M.E. had to jog along at Cody's side to keep up with her long strides.

"We'll talk to Quinn and Luke at recess and

find out what this is all about," Cody said. "I'm sure Quinn is up to something." Quinn often left cryptic notes for them, usually to arrange meetings at the clubhouse after school. No doubt this was another of his puzzles to solve, summoning the kids together.

"Wait a minute," M.E. said. "We don't have recess today. We're going to Alcatraz!"

"Oh yeah, I forgot," Cody said. "Well, we can talk to them on the bus ride over. Maybe the message has something to do with the field trip—like that e-mail I got last night."

She suddenly felt a chill run down her spine. It could have been the cold, but she suspected it was something else.

What if the notes weren't from Quinn or Luke?

# Chapter 3

Cody pulled out the two messages and studied them in class, while Ms. Stadelhofer—Ms. Stad, as the kids called her—took roll.

Cody was usually good at solving codes and puzzles, but this one had her stumped—and frustrated. If it came from Quinn, he'd be pleased that she hadn't been able to decipher the message.

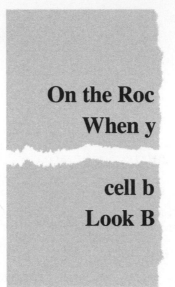

On the Roc
When y

cell b
Look B

But if it wasn't from Quinn . . .

She looked it over again. Were some letters missing? Words missing? Why was the letter B capitalized one time but not the other time? Why were the letters *y* and *B* spaced by themselves?

Cody couldn't wait to meet up with Quinn and Luke to see if they had other parts to the message.

"Class," Ms. Stadelhofer said in her attention-getting voice. Her puffy brown hair framed her round face, and her blue eyes matched her themed vest—the San Francisco city skyline, complete with an embroidered Alcatraz resting under the Golden Gate Bridge. "Do you all have your permission slips? Lunches? Money for souvenirs?"

Cody could tell everyone was excited about the field trip to Alcatraz. The prison had once been home to the infamous gangsters Al "Scarface" Capone, Alvin "Creepy" Carpis, and Diamond Dave. Cody loved the gangsters' nicknames. They were kind of like the Code Busters' code names— Kuel-Dude for Luke (Kuel was an anagram of his first name), Lock&Key for Quinn (his last name was Kee), Em-me for M.E., and CodeRed for Cody's name and her red hair.

She'd once seen a movie on TV about Robert Stroud, the "Birdman of Alcatraz," who had raised birds in his prison cell. While he had seemed like a gentle animal lover, he had also been a violent killer. *How could someone so evil be so kind to birds?* she'd wondered. When she asked her mother about him, not even Mrs. Jones could explain the Birdman's two-sided personality. That was a *real* mystery.

"Students," Ms. Stad said, pulling Cody out of her thoughts. "Please say hello to the parents who have so kindly agreed to chaperone our trip to Alcatraz." The teacher gestured toward the classroom door as four parents shuffled into the room—two women (one who looked familiar) and two men. Cody caught her breath when she saw the last parent enter.

"Dad!" she shrieked. Everyone in class turned to her. She blushed.

He waved at her. Her face turned even hotter, and she tried to shrink back into her desk.

What was he doing here? He hadn't said a word about coming! A little warning would have been nice. Cody wasn't sure she liked the idea of her father tagging along. What if she did something wrong and got in trouble, right in front of him?

Or worse, what if *he* did something to embarrass her, like tell one of his lame jokes or argue with the teacher like he did in court? Although he was an attorney, her dad could be a goofball sometimes. And he had a tendency to hover when she needed some space.

Cody turned around and gave M.E. a wide-eyed look of desperation. M.E. got the message and pressed her lips together sympathetically. Oh, well. She'd just have to make the best of it. She only hoped he didn't try to hold her hand when they crossed the street or use his pet nickname for her—"Punkin."

After Ms. Stad introduced each parent, she told the students to put on their name tags and line up at the door. Once everyone was quiet, she led the single-file line to the bus. The parents brought up the rear. Halfway to the bus Cody stepped out of line to let the other students go by and waited until her dad caught up with her.

"Dad!" she whispered. "Why didn't you tell me you were coming?"

"Hi, Punkin," he said. He'd called her that ever since she was a baby, thanks to her red hair. Punkin was also the name she'd given a cat she'd rescued from Skeleton Man's house, hoping her dad would stop calling her that. So far it hadn't worked.

"Don't call me that!" she said, glancing around to see whether anyone had heard him.

Mr. Jones grinned. "Sorry, I promise to behave. I didn't tell you because I wanted to surprise you."

"Well, you did!" Cody's green eyes flared.

"You know," her dad said, "I took a trip to Alcatraz when I was a kid, many years ago. I thought it would be interesting to see the place again. Back then it was pretty spooky. It made me think about how awful it must have been for the prisoners— cold, damp, foggy, isolated. I had nightmares about solitary confinement after that trip. In fact, it's one of the reasons why I became a public defender."

Cody's discomfort at having her dad along softened. She was proud of him—he'd kept a lot of innocent people out of prison, while her mom had put a lot of criminals behind bars. She just wished he'd stop hovering over her and stop calling her "Punkin" in front of other people.

They climbed aboard the big yellow bus. Ms. Stad told them to sit wherever they wanted for the ride over, rather than assigning them seats. "After all," she said, "this is supposed to be fun as well as educational, so as long as you behave, you may sit with your friends. Otherwise, it's back to alphabetical order."

M.E. had saved Cody a seat, right in front of Luke and Quinn, whose teacher was Mr. de Lannoy. Cody couldn't wait to show them the messages she and M.E. had received. As soon as the bus left the school parking lot, she pulled out the notes and turned to show them to the boys.

"Look what we found on our front porches," Cody said softly so the other kids sitting nearby wouldn't hear. Luckily, Matt the Brat had taken a seat at the front of the bus and was currently annoying the bus driver. "Did you do this, Quinn?" She passed the notes over to him so he could have a closer look.

Quinn's eyes widened as he glanced over the messages. He rustled through his backpack until he found what he was looking for—another folded note. Excited, Cody looked it over. It, too, was torn, this time at the top and left side.

**lock B**
**tween 2 seats**

"'Lock B? Tween two seats?'" Cody said.

"Yeah, I know," Quinn said. "It makes about as much sense as yours."

Luke pulled a piece of paper from a pocket in his oversized skater shorts and smoothed it open.

"I got one, too. But it's even more confusing than yours." He showed it to the others. This one was torn on the left side like Quinn's, but at the bottom instead of the top.

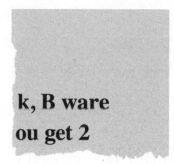

**k, B ware**
**ou get 2**

"Sound like anything to you?" Luke asked.

"Look," Cody said, pointing to the papers. "All four notes have two torn sides. Obviously, these are part of the same note. Let's piece them together."

Quinn got out a notebook to use as a flat surface and placed his piece of paper on it. He set Cody's note next to it and tried to match the two torn sides. No match. He moved his piece next to M.E.'s.

"They go together!" M.E. squealed.

"Shh!" Quinn said. He took Luke's piece and lined it up next to Cody's. Another match.

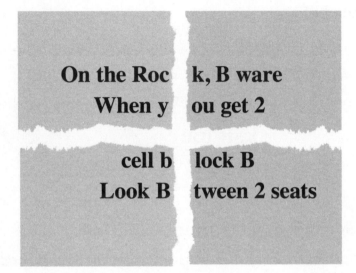

On the Roc   k, B ware
When y   ou get 2

cell b   lock B
Look B   tween 2 seats

Luke read it aloud, running some of the separated letters together to form words:

*"On the Rock, B ware*

*When you get 2 cell block B*

*Look B tween 2 seats"*

"Hey," M.E. said, "it's like a haiku—that type of

poetry that comes from Japan. Each line uses a specific number of syllables—five in the first line, seven in the second, and then five again."

"So what does it mean?" Quinn asked.

"And why are there so many capital *B*s, like B ware, cell block B, and B tween?" Luke asked.

"You really sure you didn't write this, Quinn, as some sort of game?" Cody eyed him suspiciously.

"No, I swear. I found it on my porch."

Satisfied, Cody copied the message into her Code Busters notebook so she could study it more. She twisted back in her seat and read over the lines again, trying to decode the meaning.

"*On the Rock . . .*" Did that refer to Alcatraz, also known as the Rock?

"*B ware*" was obviously "beware." But why the capital *B*?

"*When you get 2 cell block B . . .*" That had to mean Alcatraz.

"*Look B tween 2 seats . . .*" Between two seats?

What kind of seats? Did it have something to do with the electric chair? Did the prison even have an electric chair? Cody shivered at the thought. That was not something Cody was eager to see on this field trip. It was just too gruesome.

Before she could work on the message some more, the bus pulled to a stop. Cody had been so absorbed in trying to decipher the note, she'd lost track of time and was surprised to see they had arrived at the parking lot of the ferry service to Alcatraz. She could smell the bay—it smelled fishy—and scrunched up her nose. Looking through the grimy school-bus window, she spotted one of the ferries that would take them to the fog-covered island. Those boats were the only way to—and from—Alcatraz prison.

"Attention, students," Ms. Stad called out. "As you leave the bus, I'll give you a puzzle to solve about some of the prisoners who lived on the Rock. They're cryptograms, which means each

38

letter has been substituted by another letter in the alphabet. Once you figure out a couple of the letters, you should be able to crack the code and read the names of the convicts, because the letter substitutes stay the same throughout the puzzle. But there's a catch. One of these guys did not spend time on Alcatraz. So after you crack the code, figure out which one doesn't belong, then give me your answer for extra credit."

"Cool," Quinn said. "This is sort of like the ABC code or Caesar's cipher, only with letters instead of numbers. Should be easy."

Cody looked at the sheet the teacher had just passed out to the students. Quinn was right; this was going to be easy. She looked at the name on top—the first name was two letters. Duh—that was obviously *AL*. She wrote the letter *A* under the *T*, then the letter *L* under the *Q*. From there, she translated all the *T* and *Q* letters to *A* and *L*. Letter by letter she solved the puzzle.

TQ ETJGZO

FTEALZO KVZ BOQQX

EPOOJX ETPJLN

HLPRFTZ

RGE HTPBOP

JPODDX HGX CQGXR

*Code Buster's Key and Solution found on pp. 185, 190.*

Now, all she had to do was figure out which one of the convicts wasn't at Alcatraz. She remembered Ms. Stad talking about all of them—except one: Pretty Boy Floyd. He had to be the one missing from the Rock.

Cody glanced at her co–Code Busters. They, too, had solved the puzzle.

She handed her paper to Ms. Stad as she stepped out of the bus, then stared out at the small island and wondered about the prisoners. Alcatraz might be an interesting place to visit, but the idea of staying there permanently made Cody break out into goose bumps.

# Chapter 4

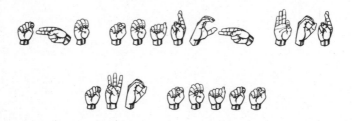

The fishy smell grew stronger as Cody stepped off the bus at Pier 33 in San Francisco. Berkeley had its unique odors, mostly ethnic foods that represented the city's cultural diversity, but nothing like this. She zipped up her jacket, pulled her hood over her head, and stuck her hands into her pockets. *Brrr.* The wind coming off the bay chilled her to the bone, and she wished she'd worn a heavier jacket.

Joining her three friends on the dock, Cody got in the ferry line with the rest of her class. The sign read ALCATRAZ TOURS, and Cody felt a rush of excitement at the thought that they would soon be at the prison. Glancing around for her dad, she saw him talking with another parent—a blonde woman who looked familiar, but Cody couldn't place her. At least she was keeping him busy.

"Let's get a spot at the front of the ferry so we have a good view on the way over," Quinn said, pulling on his baseball cap. Luke already had his hood up, ready to face the cold and wind, while M.E. had wrapped a multicolored, hand-knitted muffler around her face, head, and neck, leaving only her brown eyes visible. As for Cody, she could almost feel her curly red hair curling even more, thanks to the dampness in the air. Good thing she had put her hair in a ponytail, or those curls would look like a giant fiery ball of coils.

One of the dockworkers released the chain to the ferry, and the students began the walk up the rickety gangplank. The Code Busters tried to ease ahead past the rest of the crowd and grab the best spots for viewing, but once they arrived at the bow of the ferry, Cody's face fell.

Matt the Brat was already there.

"I beat ya!" he said. His breath smelled of peanut butter.

"We weren't racing," Luke said, pulling up next to him. Cody stood next to Luke, with M.E. and Quinn on the other side. She tried to ignore the class bully, who no doubt would try to get the Code Busters into trouble. She promised herself not to take his bait, and instead she focused on the sight of the island looming ahead, surrounded by rapidly disappearing fog. *What a cold, desolate place,* Cody thought as the wind whipped at her face.

Someone tapped Cody on the back. She turned

to see Matt grinning at her.

Again, Cody wondered if Matt had been the one who'd written the cryptic message. Cody shook her head. Besides the fact that he'd never write a poem, his spelling was atrocious, his typing was full of errors, and he would never be able to create a code like that. There was no way he could have written the secret message that the Code Busters had received.

But who else knew they were going to the Rock? Ms. Stad? Her classmates? The bus driver? They were all unlikely suspects. Anyone else?

And what did the message mean?

The ferry picked up speed, and the wind swept through Cody's clothes. Her cheeks grew numb from the icy chill. A spray of water suddenly loomed up from the bay, catching Matt directly in the face.

The Code Busters stifled their laughter, knowing it would only make Matt mad. The sight of the island emerging from the fog distracted Cody from Matt, the spray of water, and the freezing temperature. The place looked depressing, even a little dangerous, sitting in the middle of what seemed like nowhere. As they got closer, she spotted the lighthouse—she had a picture of it in her collection—and wondered if they would be allowed to go up inside. Next she recognized the three-story cell block from the pictures Ms. Stad had shown in class. Before she knew it, the ferry docked.

"Welcome to Alcatraz!" said a small Asian woman wearing an olive-green uniform and a wide Stetson hat, using a bullhorn. "My name is Jodie Huynh and I'm a ranger here on the Rock." Her name was spelled HUYNH on her name tag, but she pronounced it "Win." "You are about to enter Alcatraz Federal Prison exactly the same way the prisoners did many years ago, via the gangplank. After you arrive on the dock, please meet your teachers and the rest of your class in the designated areas."

Cody found Ms. Stadelhofer waving her arms in an area off to the side. She headed over with M.E., while Quinn and Luke met their class and Mr. de Lannoy in another area. Mr. Jones was one of the last to lumber down the gangplank a few moments later; he waved to her. Cody acknowledged him with a small smile.

*So far, so good,* she thought.

"Hello, students from Berkeley Cooperative Middle School," Ranger Huynh said through the bullhorn. Everyone quieted down. "As I mentioned, I'm a park ranger here on Alcatraz, and I'll also be your tour guide today. Before we begin the tour, I want to tell you a few things about the prison. After the tour, which will take about an hour, you'll be free to explore the island, except for the restricted areas, so watch for signs. Some of the buildings are very old, and some of the walls could come crumbling down at any time. That's part of the reason the prison was finally closed. But we'll talk more about that on the tour."

Cody looked at M.E., her eyes wide. "Cool! We get to look around on our own," she whispered. "Maybe we'll find out what that note is about."

M.E. nodded. "I'll bet this place is full of hidden passageways and secret messages left behind by the prisoners."

The ranger continued. "For nearly thirty years, from 1934 to 1963, Alcatraz Island was the most notorious federal prison in the United States. We had many famous prisoners here—Al Capone, Machine Gun Kelly, and the Birdman, Robert Stroud. The prisoners are gone, but we get about a million visitors a year—and lots of birds. This is both a park and a bird sanctuary. The island may look small, but there are more than twenty-five acres here, home to salamanders, cormorants, deer mice, pigeons, gulls, harbor seals, and herons. It may also appear far away from the city, but it's only one and a half miles from Fisherman's Wharf."

*I'm a good swimmer*, Cody thought. *I wonder if I could swim that far?*

Ranger Huynh seemed to read her mind. "But don't be tempted to dive in and swim for shore. You'd probably die of hypothermia within minutes."

Cody shivered.

"In a few moments we'll walk up the hill to Cell Block B, the main cell house. It's a steep climb, so be prepared. The fog is lifting, so be sure to check out the views of San Francisco, Marin, Berkeley, and Oakland. Everyone ready? All right then, follow me. And watch your step. Remember what I said about the birds."

Matt chanted, "Bird poop! Bird poop! Cody stepped in bird poop!"

"I did not!" Cody said. Just then Matt accidentally stepped in a big pile of bird droppings.

"Yuck! Gross!" he yelled, lifting his untied sneaker to examine the damage. One of the chaperones came over and helped him clean the bottom of the shoe by wiping it on the path.

Matt glared at Cody, as if it had been her fault. She ignored him as best she could, and tried to listen to Ranger Huynh spout off information and facts about the island as they walked up the hill. Cody caught bits and pieces that snagged her interest, mostly stuff about all the movies, TV shows, books, and games that had featured Alcatraz over the years. As they neared the cell house, she began to get a real sense of the loneliness the prisoners must have felt, locked up and isolated from society.

"Students," Ms. Stad called out after her class had assembled in front of Cell Block B. She began passing out papers with a map on one side and a list of questions on the other. "While you're here on the island, see if you can answer all the questions about Alcatraz listed on the back of your maps."

Some of the students groaned, not expecting to have to do any real work while on the trip.

Ms. Stad continued. "I'll collect your papers at the end of the trip, and if you get all the questions correct, you'll win a prize—a coupon you can use at the gift shop."

Groans turned to cheers as the students rallied to the challenge. Ms. Stad sometimes made learning fun when she turned it into a game—with prizes. Cody looked over the map and located the major landmarks—the main cell house, the lighthouse, the warden's home, the water tower, and the guards' cottages. She wondered what it would have been like to grow up living on the island, say, if her dad had been a prison guard back then. *Scary*, she thought. Ms. Stad had told the class that some of the prisoners had escaped—although none permanently. They'd either died trying or were recaught and returned to Alcatraz.

She flipped the paper over and scanned the questions on the back. They sounded pretty easy, especially since Ms. Stad had given the answers using alphanumeric code. She was very familiar with the code, where each number of the alphabet was replaced with its corresponding number—1 was A, 2 was B, and so on.

How big was the average prison cell?

**Answer: 6-9-22-5 feet by 14-9-14-5 feet.**

What did the cells contain?

**Answer: 19-9-14-11, 3-15-20, and 20-15-9-12-5-20.**

How many cells were there?

**Answer: C-C-F and F 19-15-12-9-20-1-18-25.**

Were prisoners allowed visitors?

**Answer: 25-5-19, 15-14-5   16-5-18   13-15-14-20-8.**

Why was the prison finally closed?

**Answer: 20-15-15   5-24-16-5-14-19-9-22-5 and 18-21-14 4-15-23-14.**

What was the "Rule of Silence"?

**Answer: 16-18-9-19-15-14-5-18-19 3-15-21-12-4-14'20   20-1-12-11, so they used a 20-1-16-16-9-14-7   3-15-4-5.**

How many prisoners escaped from Alcatraz?

**Answer: C-F 20-18-9-5-4 , but 14-15-14-5 23-5-18-5 19-21-3-3-5-19-19-6-21-12.**

Are there secret passageways or escape tunnels on Alcatraz?

**Answer: 25-5-19. They were 2-21-9-12-20 2-25 19-15-12-4-9-5-18-19.**

*Code Buster's Key and Solution found on pp. 185, 190.*

Cody got out her pencil and began translating the coded answers. She wondered what she'd use her coupon for in the gift shop.

"All right, everyone!" Ranger Huynh said as the students gathered around her at the entrance to the cell house. "Are you ready to go to prison?"

A few kids laughed, a few made faces, and a few yelled, "Yeah!" Cody shook her head at the students trying to sound brave—mostly boys. *Make them spend a few minutes in solitary confinement,* she thought, *and they wouldn't be so quick to act tough.*

The ranger led the way inside as the students,

teachers, and chaperones followed. If Cody thought she was cold earlier, she now felt a different kind of chill as she hurried through the steel doors. It felt as if a ghost had passed through her.

"This is the main hallway," the ranger said, "known as Broadway." Cody gazed at the cell block—two stories high, with long rows of cells on either side of both levels. She noticed how small the cells were, with only a sink, a cot, and a toilet. How could anyone live this way for years and years?

Ranger Huynh continued her patter, often surprising Cody with tidbits of information—the size of the cells (at five feet by nine feet each, they were smaller than her bathroom), how many cells there were (336), and the average length of stay (eight years!). She jotted down notes and answered questions on the paper as she listened, but when one of the students asked if the prisoners ever received visitors (yes, once a month) or letters (yes, but they were screened), her attention drifted back to the message she and the Code Busters had received that morning.

She pulled out her notebook and reread what she had copied earlier on the bus ride over: "On the Rock B ware, When you get 2 cell block B, Look B tween 2 seats."

According to the ranger, they were currently in Cell Block B—on the Rock—both mentioned in the message. But where were the "2 seats" referred to in the note? And what were they supposed to find "B tween" them?

Quinn and Luke sidled over to Cody and M.E.

"Looking for clues?" Quinn whispered.

Cody nodded. "We're in Cell Block B, but I don't see any seats. The cells just have cots, no chairs. Any ideas?"

Quinn wandered on ahead of the tour, peering into each cell as he passed by. Cody watched him until he reached the end of the long hallway. He signaled to her and the others to follow him.

Cody slowly wove her way through the crowd of students, hoping not to attract any attention, especially from Ms. Stad or her father, who was keeping a close eye on her. *Is he worried I might get lost in the cavernous cell block?* M.E. and Luke trailed behind her. When they reached Quinn, he pointed down a short hallway to the side that led to the dining area. Cody spotted two folding chairs that sat along the wall, no doubt meant for anyone who needed to rest during the tour.

Quinn glanced at the ranger, who was talking about the daily routine of the prisoners. Cody checked to make sure her dad and Ms. Stad weren't watching them.

"Luke, stand guard," Quinn said to Luke.

Quinn gestured for the others to follow, and the three of them tiptoed over to the two chairs.

Quinn bent down and examined them, including looking underneath.

"There's nothing here," he said, standing up.

"They're just chairs."

"Guys!" Luke whispered from his post.

"Cody! M.E.!" a sharp voice called from behind him.

Too late. Ms. Stad stood with her arms crossed, a frown on her usually pleasant face. Behind her stood Cody's father.

"Stay with the group," Ms. Stadelhofer said. "You can explore on your own later."

Cody nodded, and shot an apologetic glance at her father. "Sorry, Ms. Stad. We were just . . . excited about seeing everything."

"Well, you'll get a chance. Now go back with the others, or you won't be able to complete your questionnaire. You, too, boys."

The Code Busters shuffled back to the group, not so much upset about being caught but rather more disappointed that they hadn't found anything special "between the seats." Cody tried not to make eye contact with her dad.

She wondered if they'd missed something in their hurry to examine the chairs and thought about sneaking back when she heard the ranger say the word *code*. Her ears pricked up.

"It was called the 'Rule of Silence,'" the ranger was saying, "and for many years the prisoners weren't allowed to talk to each other, except during meals and recreation periods. So they used a primitive form of communication by tapping on the metal bars of their cells or on the pipes under their sinks or sometimes even on the walls."

"What was the code they used?" Luke asked.

"Good question," Ranger Huynh said. She passed out small squares of paper that featured a six-by-six grid of letters to the students. Across the top and down the side were the numbers from one to five. The alphabet letters had been written in each square of the grid, beginning with *A* and ending with *Z*.

"This is called a tap code," the ranger said. "It's one

of several codes that prisoners used, such as writing with cell-made invisible ink, and even sudoku."

## TAP CODE

|   | 1 | 2 | 3 | 4 | 5 |
|---|---|---|---|---|---|
| 1 | A | B | C | D | E |
| 2 | F | G | H | I | J |
| 3 | L | M | N | O | P |
| 4 | Q | R | S | T | U |
| 5 | V | W | X | Y | Z |

Quinn's hand shot up before several other hands. "There's no letter *K*," he said.

"Good catch!" the ranger said. "You're right. The prisoners kept the code very simple. They used the letter *C* to represent *K*. Each letter was communicated by tapping two numbers—the first one from the vertical column of numbers, and the second from the horizontal row of numbers. The letter X was used to break up sentences. So for example, if you wanted to communicate the letter Q you tapped four times, paused for a split second, then tapped once again."

Before the kids could ask questions, the sound of metal hitting metal split the air. It was so loud that M.E. jumped and grabbed Cody's arm. There were four more taps, just as loud.

"What was that?" several students asked, glancing around nervously.

The ranger grinned. "Shh! Listen . . ."

Two more taps broke the silence. Then a longer pause.

A tap, then a tap.

Four taps, then four more.

One tap, then five.

Four taps, then two.

*Code Buster's Solution found on p. 191.*

"Water!" Quinn shouted. "Someone just tapped out the word *water.*"

"Very good!" Ranger Huynh said. "Now, if you look up there"—she pointed to the second floor—"you'll see Geoff, one of our guards here on Alcatraz, holding a big wrench. He just tapped out the code for *water.*"

"That was cool!" Cody said. She looked up at the elderly uniformed man above her. He wore a gray, double-breasted jacket and slacks, black shoes, a hat with a badge in front, and a bright red tie.

"Why didn't they just use Morse code?" Luke asked.

"Morse code is a lot harder to send by tapping," the ranger said, "because you have to create two different tap sounds—a *dih* and a *dah* sound. And it takes time to memorize the code. The tap code is easier to learn and simpler to decode.

"By the way, you kids didn't invent the texting code you use with your cell phones. The prisoners used acronym shortcuts all the time. For example, they tapped out *GN* for 'good night' or *TY* for 'thank you.'"

Quinn reached over to the wall next to him and tapped "1-3, 3-4, 3-4, 3-1."

*Code Buster's Solution found on p. 191.*

The ranger smiled at Quinn. "Great! You figured it out. You might want to join the park rangers someday and give this tour yourself."

"Nah," Quinn said. "I'm going to join the CIA."

# Chapter 5

WHAT IS IT?

"Sweet. Even the prisoners used codes," Luke said. He and Quinn did a knuckle bump.

"There must be a million ways to create codes and secret languages," Quinn added. "I'll never learn them all! Right now, I'm trying to learn Egyptian hieroglyphs and the runic alphabet."

"All right, everyone," the ranger called on her bullhorn. "Please follow me into the dining hall.

That's where the prisoners ate their meals. It was affectionately called 'the gas chamber,' thanks to all the beans that were served." The students giggled. "You'll find a map of the cell house on the back of the tap code sheet."

The students shuffled through the hallway where Quinn had discovered the two chairs that had turned out to be false clues. Cody saw him linger, giving the seats a last look, then he followed her and the rest of his classmates into the dining area. The large room was empty, except for some long benches that remained in the back. Cody imagined school-cafeteria-type tables with hungry prisoners sitting on the benches, hunching over their food trays. She wondered if they had the same type of cafeteria food their school had, like sloppy joes, fish sticks, and greasy pizza. She had a feeling it wasn't much different.

"The food here at Alcatraz was supposed to be the best in the entire prison system," Ranger

Huynh announced. "Each prisoner was assigned a row and a seat, such as A-1, A-2, and so on. They had only twenty minutes to eat, and gobbled the food up quickly before other prisoners could steal from their trays."

Cody had a sudden thought. The ranger had said the rows and seats were lettered and numbered. Maybe the torn message they'd received earlier referred to seats in the dining hall, rather than chairs, like they'd first suspected. As the large group of students followed the ranger to the kitchen area beyond, Cody waited until her dad was inside and out of sight, then she waved the other Code Busters back toward the benches.

"S'up?" Luke asked, watching the rest of the crowd file into the next room.

"The benches!" Cody said softly so the group wouldn't hear. "I think that's what the message meant. Remember how the letter *B* stood out from the other letters? And the number two was mentioned a couple of times? Maybe they refer to Seat B-Two in the dining hall."

"Let's check it out before Stad and Mr. de Lannoy notice we're missing," Quinn said.

*And my dad*, Cody thought.

Quinn ran over to the second row of benches, the others right behind him. "This is Row B," he said, and he pointed to the second seat. "And here's Seat Two."

Luke leaned over for a closer look. "Nothing here, dude, except some scratches. Probably carved by the prisoners with their forks."

Cody shook her head. "They didn't have metal utensils."

"No, but some did have shivs," Quinn said.

M.E. scrunched her nose. "What's a shiv?"

"Like a homemade knife," Quinn answered. "Prisoners use anything they can, like a toothbrush handle or broken comb, and sharpen it to a point.

I saw a picture online that was made from a pork chop bone."

"Yikes," Cody said. The thought of a shiv made her shiver. "Wouldn't want to be stabbed with a pork chop bone."

"I wouldn't want to be stabbed with anything," M.E. added.

Luke knelt down and peered under the bench. His eyes widened, and he reached underneath.

"You found something!" Cody said, excited. "What is it?"

He pulled a small piece of paper from the underside of the bench. Remnants of clear tape were still stuck to it.

"A note!" M.E. squealed, then clapped her mouth shut.

"Shh!" Quinn reminded her. He glanced into the next room, hoping the teachers hadn't heard them.

"Open it!" Cody whispered.

Luke unfolded the white sheet of paper, looked at it, then held it up for the others to see.

( 4 /\/ |) |_ 3   () /\/   + # 3   VV 4 + 3 |2

*Code Buster's Key and Solution found on pp. 186, 191.*

"I don't get it," he said, after scanning the message. "What's it supposed to mean?"

Quinn took it from Luke's hand. "Hey, I recognize this code. Online gamers and hackers use it when they don't want just anybody reading their messages. They call it LEET code, or 1337, which is LEET written backward and upside down. It uses numbers and symbols to make letters."

"How do you decode it?" Cody asked, studying the message.

"It's pretty easy. Just sound it out phonetically. Watch." Quinn took out a ballpoint pen and his notebook from his backpack, and wrote: (,) (_) ! /\/ /\/ "What do you see?"

"I see some parentheses, a comma, a dash, an

exclamation mark ..."

"Okay, now think of the symbols and numbers as alphabet letters."

She deciphered the first letter. "That looks like a Q," she said aloud. "Then *U*. Then *I N N*. Quinn!"

"Right. So now try to read the words on the other side."

"You've already figured it out?" Cody asked him. He nodded. She flipped the paper and studied the first series of numbers and symbols.

( 4 /\/ |) |_ 3

The first symbol resembled the letter *C*. She wrote the letter underneath the symbol. Next came the number *4*. What letter did it look like? Sort of an *A*. She jotted it next to the *C*. The next symbol was obvious—*N*—made with diagonal lines. The letters *D* and *L* were also easy. The last letter of the first word was tricky, though. It just looked like the number *3*.

"I'm stuck," Cody said.

Quinn wrote down the number *3*, then held it upside down for Cody to see. "Sometimes the letters are reversed."

"So the number *3* must be an *E*." She added the letter, then read when she'd deciphered: "Candle!"

"That's awesome," M.E. said. "Let me try the next one." She took the notebook and the pen from Cody and studied the next two symbols: () /\/

"Oh, it's an easy one," she said. "It has to be 'on.'"

"My turn," Luke said. He borrowed the pen and notebook and went to work on the next word: + # 3. "The plus sign looks like the letter *T*. The pound sign—it kind of looks like the letter *H*. And *3* means *E*. It spells 'the.'"

"Quinn, you want to finish it?" Cody asked.

Quinn nodded and took the notebook and pen from Luke. "There are two *V*s, which make *W*. Then the number *4*, which is an *A*. The plus sign means *T*; *3* means *E*—"

"R!" Cody said. "It's made with a *1* and a *2*, side by side. It spells *water.*"

"'Candle on the water'?" Luke read the decoded message. "Okay, what's *that* supposed to mean?"

M.E.'s eyes brightened. "Hey, did you ever see that old movie *Pete's Dragon?*"

The others shook their heads.

"What's a dragon got to do with this?" Quinn asked.

"In the movie," M.E. explained, "there was this orphan kid named Pete who found an invisible dragon. A lighthouse keeper and his daughter take him in because bad guys are chasing him. Anyway, when a storm comes, the lamp at the lighthouse goes out, so the dragon lights it again with his fire and saves the ships out at sea."

"I still don't see—" Quinn interrupted.

"The lady in the movie sang a song called 'Candle on the Water,' which meant—"

Before M.E. could finish, Cody said, "Lighthouse!"

Quinn broke into a grin. "So this message is telling us to go to the lighthouse here on Alcatraz!"

Cody saw a shadow pass over the note in Quinn's hand.

"I'll take that!" Ms. Stadelhofer said, holding out her hand. Quinn handed it over.

The Code Busters—busted!

They'd been so focused on trying to solve the mysterious message, they hadn't noticed the teacher walking up behind them. "You four are supposed to be in the kitchen, following the ranger's tour! I have half a mind to send you back to the ferry for the rest of the trip."

Cody felt a wave of heat wash over her body. Standing in the doorway to the kitchen was her father. He had witnessed the whole embarrassing scene. Great. She was in trouble, and her dad knew. Was that disappointment she saw in his eyes? Or something else?

"Now get in there and don't let me catch you

wandering away again." Stad pointed to the kitchen. "Otherwise, there will be no free time for the four of you to explore the island on your own."

Quinn began clicking the ballpoint pen he still held in his hand. To anyone else, the clicking probably sounded random. But to the Code Busters' trained ears, the clicks meant something. Quinn was signaling them in Morse code:

.-- .... .- -

-.. - - -

.-- .

-.. - - -

-. - - - .- -

*Code Buster's Key and Solution found on pp. 186, 191.*

# Chapter 6

Cody and the others hurried toward the prison kitchen, where the ranger was telling more stories about prison life. She glanced at her dad as she passed him in the doorway. To her surprise, instead of looking angry, he winked at her.

What did that mean?

Slipping into the kitchen area before he could

hover, she met up with the rest of her classmates. When she looked back, he was whispering to her teacher.

Uh-oh. What was that about?

"... like to hear my favorite story about Alcatraz?" Cody caught Ranger Huynh saying, her eyes dancing with excitement. A cheer rose from the crowd.

"All right, follow me downstairs to the dungeon cells," the ranger said, waving them on. "That's where the prisoners were sent if they caused any problems while incarcerated here on the Rock."

"You mean, the Hole?" Matt the Brat shouted in Cody's ear. She fanned his peanut butter breath away from her face.

The ranger didn't seem surprised at the question. "Actually, they called those dungeon cells solitary confinement, but yes, some of the prisoners referred to it as the Hole, since it was smaller and darker than the regular prison cells."

"Al Capone died in one of them," Matt continued, grinning as if he was sharing privileged information.

"No," the ranger said, "that's not true. There are a lot of stories about Alcatraz that aren't true. It's part of my job to separate fact from fiction."

She led the group out to the main hallway, then down a flight of steel steps to what appeared to be a basement. As they moved along, Cody saw a row of closed doors. Ranger Huynh opened a thick door with her key, then Geoff, the former Alcatraz guard who had tapped out the tap code earlier, pulled a lever that caused the inner barred doors to slide open. She and Geoff opened three more cells, allowing all the students to see inside the cells.

Cody took her turn peering into the tiny room, which was no larger than a closet in her house. She shuddered. Nothing but a cot, a toilet, four walls, and a cement floor. As the students viewed the cells, most grew quiet, and others gasped. How awful it must have been there. She wondered how many men had spent time in that small, cramped space.

"Anyone brave enough to go inside?" the ranger said.

A few hands shot up, including Luke's and Matt the Brat's. Cody knew Luke was always ready to take a dare. But Matt? He was just showing off.

"All right," the ranger said. "You, you, you, and you—step inside."

Luke, Matt, a classmate named Jodie, and her twin brother, Jeffy, grinned at being selected, and walked into the tiny rooms.

"Now, how about if I close the doors," the ranger said, "so you can get the full effect?"

Jodie and Jeffy both dashed out of their cells.

"No way!" Jeffy said.

"It's creepy in there even with the door open," Jodie said.

Luke remained in the cell, his arms crossed, his jaw cocked. Matt's face grew red, and Cody could see the fear in his eyes, in spite of his bravado. Seconds later he stepped out and said, "I have claustrophobia." He wiped the sweat from his forehead with the sleeve of his jacket, ignoring the rolling eyes of the other students.

"Fear of small spaces isn't uncommon," the ranger said. "But can you imagine spending hours, days, even weeks in there?"

Cody saw Matt visibly shudder.

The ranger turned her attention to Luke, the lone survivor. "What's your name?"

"Luke LaVeau."

"Are you ready, Luke?"

Cody's eyes widened as her friend gave a single nod. She heard a creaking sound as Geoff pulled the lever to close the barred door.

"You okay?" the ranger asked.

Luke nodded. Cody saw the muscles in his crossed arms tighten.

Ranger Huynh closed the heavy outer door.

Luke disappeared from sight.

"Can you hear me in there, Luke?"

The students hushed, listening for any response from their classmate.

Nothing.

Then came the faint sound of tapping:

••• ▬ ▬ ▬ •••

*Code Buster's Key and Solution found on pp. 186, 191.*

"That's Morse code!" Cody said, frowning. "Maybe he's in trouble!"

The ranger reached for the door.

"Leave him in there!" Matt the Brat shouted, and laughed.

Cody shot him a dirty look. Ranger Huynh ignored him. She opened the door, signaled Geoff to pull back the bars, and then released the temporary prisoner.

Luke grinned proudly as he stepped out. Cody was relieved to see he was fine and just teasing them with his Morse code emergency call.

"How was it, Luke?" she asked him.

He shrugged as if it were no big deal. "Cold. Dark. Kind of weird."

"Can you imagine spending even twenty-four hours in there?"

Luke raised his eyebrows and shook his head. "No way. I'd probably lose it."

Cody cringed at the thought of spending any time inside a confined space like that. She didn't even like being alone in an elevator for more than a few seconds. Maybe she had a touch of claustrophobia, too. Being in the Hole would totally creep her out.

The ranger gave Luke a pat on the back as he moved to stand next to Quinn. "The rest of you," the ranger continued, "feel free to step inside for a few seconds, if you dare. Meanwhile, I want to tell you another one of my favorite Alcatraz stories. It began right here, in solitary confinement."

As the students took turns stepping into the small open cell, Ranger Huynh began her latest tale. "Over fifty years ago, there was a prisoner here named Diamond Dave Melvin. He was a jewel thief who tried to escape the Rock and was put in solitary confinement. Diamond Dave was known for the drawings he scratched into the walls of his prison cells."

Cody pictured the story as the ranger told it. She could just see a tall, handsome jewel thief, like the ones in movies who wore fancy suits and drove big cars by day, then changed into dark, hooded clothes and crept into houses at night.

The ranger continued. "There's one of his drawings, there." She pointed a flashlight on the back wall of the cell, revealing scratches that looked like a tall building. "Can you tell what it is?"

A few hands went up, including Luke's.

"A house?" one of the students asked.

"Close," the ranger said. "Anyone else?"

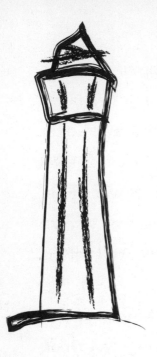

"A spaceship?" Matt asked, no doubt trying to be funny.

"Nope. I'll give you a clue. One night a man walks out of a house. As he leaves, he turns the light on instead of off. Why?"

Cody raised her hand, then gave the answer.

*Code Buster's Solution found on p. 191.*

"That's right!" the ranger said. "Unfortunately, we never found a map that he drew that would lead to the jewels he'd allegedly hidden."

"When they released him from solitary confinement," Ranger Huynh said, "they found more of his drawings. He'd carved the shapes using a sharpened edge of a food tray, and even used some of the food to draw with."

"But it was dark in there when you closed the door," Luke said.

"That's right," the ranger said. "Even though he couldn't see anything in that dark room, he used his imagination to create his lighthouses."

Cody frowned. Here was a thief who spent time on Alcatraz, yet he apparently shared a love of lighthouses, just like her. She knew about all the different parts of a lighthouse—the lamps, lenses, lantern rooms, day beacons, lightning rods. Her mother had once asked her why she loved lighthouses so much. She'd said she saw them as safe places. Her mother had given her a hug and said, "Don't worry, you're safe with me." But in spite of knowing that her parents would take care of her, she still liked the idea of a place where everything was peaceful, even during a storm.

The ranger continued her story. "Diamond Dave seemed to be obsessed with the lighthouse on Alcatraz. He could see it from the exercise yard, and the guards said he used to stare at it for hours. When the bell rang for the prisoners to come in, he was always the last one inside. That lighthouse was built to warn sailors of dangers in the fog-shrouded waters of San Francisco Bay. But for Diamond Dave, I think it was a symbol of freedom. What do you all think?"

While the students raised their hands and offered answers, Cody's mind drifted. She wondered if the lighthouse might have symbolized something more than freedom for Diamond Dave . . . such as the hiding place for his diamonds? But if that was true, how could the jewels have made it to Alcatraz without being found by the guards? And if they had been hidden in the lighthouse, they probably would have been found by now.

Her mind immediately jumped to the note they'd found under Seat B-2 in the dining hall. It had read: "Candle on the Water."

A lighthouse.

"Whatever happened to Diamond Dave?" Quinn asked.

"He was finally released, after serving his time," the ranger answered. "Then he just disappeared. No one ever saw him again. Rumor has it that he reclaimed the diamonds his buddies had hidden for him, following clues they'd left while visiting him in prison. But no one knows where the diamonds—or Dave—ended up. He could have died before finding his treasure. He could have been double-crossed by his so-called pals. Or he could have found the diamonds, left the country, and lived out his days in style. It's one of those unsolved mysteries that makes Alcatraz so interesting."

Cody looked at Quinn, then Luke, then M.E. Their eyes were wide.

"All right, everyone, this concludes the tour," the ranger said. "Feel free to visit the gift shop and explore the rest of the island, as long as you stay out of the restricted areas."

"Are you thinking what I'm thinking?" Quinn whispered to the other three.

They nodded, grinning.

M.E. stuck out her index finger. "The e-mail you got on your computer, Cody," she said, raising another finger, and another, and another, as she listed the clues. "The torn messages we found on our front porches. The clue we found under the bench. The story of Diamond Dave and his drawings."

Cody was about to blurt out the key to the clues M.E. had just listed when she noticed Matt the Brat standing nearby, obviously trying to overhear them. She raised her finger to her lips to silence the others, then finger-spelled what she'd been about to say:

*Code Buster's Key and Solution found on pp. 184, 191.*

"It has to be that!" Quinn said. "So let's go!"

# Chapter 7

ust a sec," Cody said, as they began to head for
the lighthouse. She ducked into the gift shop
and helped herself to a free brochure. Returning
a few moments later, she showed the brochure to
the others.

Quinn said, "We already have a map."

"I know," she said, unfolding it, "but I want to

see if there's anything more about the lighthouse. Maybe there's a secret entrance or something." Cody read it over.

"What's it say?" M.E. asked.

Cody skimmed it for information to share. "Ummm . . . built in 1854 . . . automated in 1963— the year the prison was closed. It's still a working lighthouse . . . first one on the West Coast . . . built of reinforced concrete . . . octagon-shaped . . . eighty-four feet high . . ."

"Skip the boring stuff," Luke interrupted. "Is there anything we really need to know?"

Cody frowned at him. "Only that the grounds aren't open to the public, so we can't go in it."

Quinn shot her a look of concern.

"But we'll see when we get there," Cody said. "There should be a sign."

They climbed the steep hill leading to the lighthouse, which looked like a giant chess piece. Cody continued to read the rest of the brochure to make sure she hadn't missed anything.

"Did you know the lighthouse also had a fog bell that helped keep ships from running into the island?" she asked. "And sailors used signals and codes to call for help in times of trouble. For example, they communicated over the airwaves using the phonetic alphabet. Each letter matched a word, so sailors could clearly understand the call. See if you can translate this example":

Sierra – Hotel – India – Papa

India – November

Delta – India – Sierra – Tango – Romeo – Echo – Sierra – Sierra

*Code Buster's Key and Solution found on pp. 187, 191.*

Cody was about to give the answer when Luke suddenly jerked her arm, startling her.

"Hey!" she said, still annoyed at him for interrupting her earlier.

Luke pointed to the white pile she was about to step in. "Watch where you step. There's bird poop everywhere."

Cody glanced around. Luke was right—it was all over the place. She'd been so involved in reading the brochure she hadn't been watching where she was walking. Yuck. Her shoes would have been ruined if she'd stepped in that stuff.

As they neared the lighthouse, Cody glanced at the view from atop the hill. Since the fog had lifted, she could see all the way to Berkeley. *Wow, she thought, it's beautiful from up here.*

"There's the door," Quinn said. "And it's open," he said, wide-eyed.

Cody nodded toward a sign Quinn had apparently missed. "But it's off-limits. See the sign? NO ADMITTANCE. AUTHORIZED PERSONNEL ONLY."

"But the door's open," he protested.

"Hey, what are you kids doing?" a man's voice sounded from behind them.

Cody and the others spun around. She recognized Geoff, the old guard who had been assisting Ranger Huynh on the tour. He stood behind them, hands on his hips, frowning. Unlike the ranger, who'd worn the park uniform, Geoff wore a traditional prison guard's uniform—gray, with a red tie and round cap.

"Nothing," Quinn said, pulling back from the lighthouse door.

"Can't go inside," Geoff the guard said. "Staff only. Too dangerous, especially for kids."

"We were just . . . checking it out," Luke offered. "The ranger said we could go exploring."

"Yeah, but not inside the lighthouse. Didn't you see the sign?"

None of the kids said anything.

The hard frown on the man's face softened. "You're that kid who solved the tap code, aren't you?" he asked Quinn.

Quinn nodded proudly.

"I heard you kids talking. You're on some kind of treasure hunt or something, aren't you?"

"Not really a treasure hunt," Quinn said. "We're . . ." He glanced at the others. "We're just curious about the lighthouse." He indicated Cody. "She collects lighthouse pictures."

"Remembered the story of Diamond Dave?"

The Code Busters grinned and nodded.

*This guy knows what we're up to,* Cody thought.

"Yeah, that story always fascinated me, too. So you really want to see inside, huh?" the guard asked, readjusting his cap.

Quinn's eyebrows rose. "Sure!"

"All right. If you just want a quick look. You gotta be careful, though. No fooling around. And just go up and come straight down. Got me?"

"Awesome! We'll be careful," Luke said, obviously excited.

Cody wasn't so sure. There was probably a reason the public wasn't allowed in the lighthouse.

It really could be dangerous. What if there was another earthquake? The whole place could come crumbling down.

Quinn seemed to notice Cody's reluctance and nudged her. "You okay?" he whispered. "This is going to be cool."

Cody nodded, not wanting to appear scared. M.E. was usually the reluctant one, but this time she felt anxious.

"Go on in," the guard said. "But like I told you, be careful. And hurry. You got five minutes. And if you find the diamonds, we split fifty-fifty." He grinned at them.

Quinn led the way in through the door, while Cody brought up the rear. As soon as she entered the small, octagonal room, she was glad she'd come. Right in the middle was a black iron spiral staircase that twisted its way up to the top. Graffiti was scratched and penned on the inside walls of the room, and Cody read several slogans from a group called the American Indian Movement, which had taken over the island years before: CUSTER HAD IT COMING and TAKE BACK AMERICA.

"Wow," M.E. said, glancing around. Cody held tightly to the curved railing of the creaky metal staircase as they began their ascent.

"Look for some kind of message," Quinn said. Cody had nearly forgotten why they were here—to find a message. Well, if there was a message waiting for them inside this lighthouse, then someone who had a key must have put it there. Matt the Brat wouldn't have had access. And if it wasn't Matt, who could it be?

Or was this just a wild-goose chase?

As soon as they reached the top of the staircase, Cody felt the wind whip through slats in the tower, burning her eyes, but she was so dazzled by the thick glass windows that surrounded them, she hardly noticed. A huge beacon of bright light in the center of the tiny room turned a sweeping 360 degrees, sending its powerful light to all parts of the bay.

"Whoa," she whispered to herself. This was the first time she'd seen the inside of a real lighthouse. It truly was awesome. And the view was even more breathtaking.

"Look for a message!" Quinn said again as they moved around inside the tower.

The kids began searching for some clue related to the mysterious note they'd found in the prison dining hall. They checked the walls, the floor, the ceiling, the light itself. But five minutes later, they'd come up empty-handed.

"There's nothing here," Luke said, taking a last look around. "And it's freezing."

"Time's up," the guard called from below, his voice echoing up through the cement tower.

"Let's go." Luke started down the twisting staircase.

Cody was about to follow him down when she

spotted something in one of the small alcoves.

"Wait." She headed over, then picked up a glass jar. "Look at this." She held it up. An old cork lay at the bottom of the jar.

Quinn took the jar from her and turned it over. The cork fell into his hand. "This looks like a home-made compass. We made these in Scouts. See the rust line at the bottom of the glass, where all the water evaporated? And the cork even has a nee-dle in it. That's how we made them—by floating a cork with a needle in water. The needle always points north."

"So you think this was a compass?" M.E. asked.

"I don't know," Quinn said. "Let's try it." He got out a bottle of water from his backpack and poured it into the small glass jar, then held it up and peered at it. The cork floated around in circles. "I don't think it's working. It needs to be magnetized."

"Hey, you kids. Come on down," the guard called again.

"We're coming!" Quinn yelled back. "Cody, where exactly did you find this?"

Cody showed him the alcove where she'd discovered the glass jar and cork. On the wall next to it was graffiti, most of it written with a black marker. But at the bottom, someone had actually carved something into the cement wall.

"Check this out," Quinn said, pointing to the markings. "It looks like some kind of code."

Cody peered at it and recognized the dots and dashes.

-.-. .- -- .-.. .- -. .. .-.. .

-... . .-.. .-..

- --- .-- . .-.

110

-.. . - -. .-. . . ...

"It's Morse code!" Cody said.

"Translate it, and I'll write it down," M.E. said,

pulling out her notepad from her backpack.

Cody read it aloud.

*Code Buster's Key and Solution found on pp. 186, 191.*

"What's that supposed to mean?" Luke said.

"Hey, kids! Do I have to come up there and get you?" the guard called again, sounding agitated.

"We're coming! We're coming!" Quinn called. He turned to the others. "Since there was a home-made compass there, maybe it refers to degrees."

Quinn thought for a moment, then said, "Anyone bring a cell phone?"

Luke, M.E., and Cody all pulled out their phones.

"How come you all got to bring your phones and I didn't?" Quinn grumbled.

"I only get to take it on special occasions, like this," Cody said.

"Me, too," M.E. said. Luke nodded.

"Not fair. Let me see your iPhone, Cody." She handed it over. Quinn switched it on and tapped the compass app. He held it up. It pointed north.

"Here's 110 degrees," he said, then looked up and out the window of the lighthouse tower. "It's pointing to the Campanile on the Berkeley campus. I can see it from here! Maybe we're supposed to go to the Campanile to find our next clue."

"When?" M.E. asked.

"Tomorrow is Saturday," Quinn said. "We can meet there in the morning."

"All right, I'm coming up there!" the guard shouted.

He didn't sound happy. It was time to get out of the lighthouse.

# Chapter 8

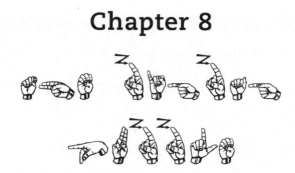

Cody was more than ready to leave the top of the icy-cold tower. With the wind whipping through the open slats, she was chilled to the bone and her teeth were chattering. She carefully followed Luke down, holding on to the twisting railing, tailed by M.E. and Quinn.

"You kids are going to get me fired," Geoff the

guard said as they touched down on the cement floor. Cody and her friends stepped through the door and out of the lighthouse, followed by the guard, who shut the door behind him.

"So did you kids find anything up there?" he asked, twisting the key. "Any diamonds?"

"Nope," Quinn said, shooting Cody a look. "Just a lot of graffiti."

It was Code Buster policy to keep stuff like that to themselves.

"There's a lot of that from when the American Indian Movement was here," Geoff said. "But no sign of a message to Diamond Dave, eh?"

The kids forced a laugh. Cody felt herself blush. "Not that we saw," Cody said.

"Okay, well, you kids run along now," Geoff said. "And by the way, it wouldn't be a good idea to mention this. Could get us all in trouble."

The kids nodded and started down the hill. But Cody turned back and caught a last glimpse of the guard standing by the lighthouse, watching them. When he spotted her looking at him, he ducked inside the door and closed it behind him. Cody thought she saw a note flapping on the outside of the door and quickly ran back to check, wondering if they had missed a clue.

When she reached the door, she saw the message written on the note. It was written in ABC code. The letters of the message were broken into groups, and each set of letters began with a sequential alphabet letter.

"Ado bes cth dis ecl fue gri hng iab jel kl?"

*Code Buster's Solution found on p. 191.*

The door jerked open.

Geoff stepped out. "I thought you kids were gone."

"I . . . I just saw this note on the door—" Cody started to say.

Geoff snatched the note off the back of the door.

"Oh, that's nothing. Bunch of jibberish left by some kid. Go on, now."

Cody nodded and followed the others down the hill to the gift shop, puzzled over the message she'd found. It had to be a message meant for the Code Busters, but the guard had snatched it out of her hands before she could read the rest.

She entered the store, hoping to find some souvenirs for her family. She especially wanted to buy one of the commemorative diamonds.

M.E. came up behind Cody as she looked at some key chains that featured pictures of the Rock.

"So do you think those coordinates actually point to the Campanile tower?" she whispered.

"Yeah," Quinn said, pulling up next to Cody. He wore a striped prison cap. Apparently, he'd overheard M.E. in spite of her whispering. "That plus the ABC code message have to be the clues. The Morse code was the only set of marks that wasn't made by a permanent marker. I doubt the prisoners had markers back in those days. If anyone wanted to leave a permanent message, he'd have to carve it. Besides, those numbers and marks didn't fit with the other graffiti."

"But why would someone randomly carve out Morse code and the coordinates for the UC tower?" Luke asked, standing behind them holding an ESCAPED FROM ALCATRAZ PSYCH WARD T-shirt.

"That's just it," Quinn answered. "It wasn't random. I think it was one of Diamond Dave's gang members. He probably came to visit Dave in prison, but he couldn't just tell him where the diamonds were hidden in case someone overheard him. So he talked about the lighthouse or brought him a picture of it—and that was a clue. Remember how Dave kept drawing lighthouses? He seemed obsessed with them. He probably knew there was a message waiting for him there when he finally got out of prison."

"We'll just have to go to the Campanile bell tower to find out," M.E. said, shrugging. "Maybe the diamonds are hidden there."

"Yeah," Quinn agreed. "We have to check. You never know. And they might still be there after all these years."

The kids spent the rest of their free time deciding what to buy. Quinn bought himself a tin cup that was painted with black and white stripes and had the word ALCATRAZ stenciled on the side. Luke got the T-shirt he was holding, and another one in a larger size for his *grand-mère*. Naturally M.E. picked out some striped Alcatraz knee-high socks to wear to school, claiming, "They go with everything!" Cody finally found a duplicate prison-cell key for her dad, an Alcatraz guard badge for her mother, an Alcatraz bookmark for her sister, Tana, and a fake diamond about the size of a walnut for herself.

On the way out of the shop, Cody spotted her dad. He stood on the dock a few feet away, talking to the same woman she had seen him with earlier. She went up to him with her bag of gifts and pulled out his key, ignoring the woman.

"I got you this," Cody said to her dad, handing him the key. It was the size of a cell phone and weighed about the same. "You can use it as a paperweight to keep on your desk and remind you to get all those innocent people out of jail."

Cody's dad glanced at the woman next to him as he took the key. "Thank you, Dakota, but you interrupted Ms. Webster and me. We were talking."

Cody blushed. She'd meant to interrupt him but didn't think he'd notice. Now she felt embarrassed.

"Cody, do you know Ms. Webster?" her dad asked.

The blonde woman reached out her hand. "Hi, Dakota. I'm Matthew's mom. We met some time ago. I don't know if you remember."

Cody's blood went cold. Matt the Brat's mom! Cody knew she'd recognized her when the chaperones had entered the classroom earlier, but she hadn't paid attention to the introductions once she'd spotted her dad. Besides, the one time she'd seen Matt's mom, the woman had had short brown hair and looked a lot heavier. This couldn't be the same woman—with blonde, shoulder-length hair and a slim figure. She didn't even have the same last name as Matt.

"You're Matt the— Matt's mom?" Cody asked, catching herself before the word *Brat* came flying out. "But his last name is Jeffreys . . ."

The woman nodded. "I changed my last name back to my maiden name when Matt's father and I divorced a few months ago."

Great. Her dad had been flirting with none other than Matt the Brat's mother, and the woman was now blonde, thin, and available. Cody had to break up this little friendship quickly, before she became Matt the Brat's stepsister!

"Dad, could I talk to you? Privately?" Cody stared at her dad, trying to will him to agree.

"Sure, Punkin." Mr. Jones glanced at Matt's mom and said, "Will you excuse us?"

The woman nodded.

"Hey, sweetheart. Are you having a good time?"

"Yeah, Dad, this place is totally cool. I just got some souvenirs for you and Mom and Tana."

"Great . . . uh . . . " her father stammered, then said, "Did anything unusual happen while you were here?"

Cody thought about the lighthouse side trip and the message found there, but said nothing. That was one of the rules of the Code Busters Club—coded messages were kept secret.

"Nope," she said, not looking her dad in the eye.

"Not even when you kids wandered off during the cafeteria talk?"

"Oh, that. Sorry. We were just curious about the benches and wanted to check them out."

Her dad patted her back.

"Well, be careful. And let me know if you need any help with anything."

*Why would I need help with anything?* Cody

wondered. "Thanks, Dad," she said.

She headed back to her friends, wondering if she should have told her dad about the message in the lighthouse. No, she decided. Nothing had happened. They hadn't been in any danger. And she wanted to follow this Diamond Dave mystery as far as it went.

On the ride home, Ms. Stad made sure Cody and M.E. were seated separately from Quinn and Luke—no doubt as punishment for their sneaking off together in the cell block during the ranger's talk. *No biggie*, Cody thought. The Code Busters had ways of communicating, even from a distance.

Sure enough, a few minutes later a folded note arrived in Cody's hands. She glanced behind her to see Quinn give a brief wave, letting her know the note was from him. She'd already guessed it was, because the paper was intricately folded— origami was something Quinn liked to do with his secret messages. This one looked like a square, but when Cody pulled out the tucked corners, the paper unfolded into a large sheet of paper. Inside, Quinn had written a code.

Cody recognized it immediately as the zigzag code, because at the very end was the letter V, which stood for "zigzag." At first glance she saw a string of random letters.

M e a t e a p n l t m r o a t n e t t h
c m a i e o o r w t e V

Since this was a zigzag code, she knew to divide the letters in half and write the second half underneath the first, after moving it one space to the right.

M e a t e a p n l t m r o a t n
  e t t h c m a i e o o r w t e

Once she'd done that, she added the zigzag lines to connect the top and bottom letters, beginning with the letter M.

*Code Buster's Solution found on p. 192.*

110

Cody shared the note with M.E. Tomorrow would be Saturday—her day to be with her dad—but she'd think of some reason she needed to meet with her friends. They'd have plenty of time to explore the Campanile tower on the Berkeley campus and see if they could find more clues to the hidden diamonds—or the diamonds themselves. The girls finger-spelled *OK* to Quinn and Luke.

Out of the corner of her eye, Cody saw a hand trying to imitate her message.

Matt. He'd caught her signal.

Uh-oh. Now that he knew the Code Busters were up to something, he'd be all up in their faces, asking questions and trying to trick them into spilling their plans.

He might even follow them to the campus . . .

Cody knew they'd better be on the lookout tomorrow, or Matt the Brat might be the one to find the lost diamonds.

# Chapter 9

Y ou're late," Quinn said, checking his military
watch. Cody had just arrived at the Campanile tower on the University of California, Berkeley, campus at two minutes past ten. She'd asked
her dad if he'd drive her to the campus to meet up
with the Code Busters for a special project they'd
been working on. She knew he'd let her go if her

plans had anything to do with schoolwork. She'd just failed to mention that this was extracurricular.

M.E. and Luke grinned at Cody. They all knew Quinn was a fanatic about time. They usually just ignored his comments.

"Sorry. My dad has been acting strangely lately. He keeps asking me weird questions, and hovering. He even asked if I wanted him to come along today," Cody said, rolling her eyes. She was dressed in jeans and a long-sleeved white T-shirt, as well as her usual red hoodie, ready for the morning chill that was rapidly burning off. She looked at M.E. in her shorts-over-tights outfit and extra-long T-shirt that featured a picture of Tigger. Nothing matched, especially not with the Alcatraz socks she'd pulled on over the tights. But Cody knew M.E. didn't care. Her friend enjoyed being different from everyone else. In Berkeley, nearly everyone seemed to have their own style.

Quinn wore khaki slacks and a button-down

madras shirt, while Luke was dressed in his usual sweats with the New Orleans Saints logo. New Orleans was Luke's hometown, but he'd moved to Berkeley to live with his *grand-mère* after the big flood. He never talked about his parents, who had died in the flood, and none of the Code Busters asked him about it.

Cody noticed a note in Quinn's hand.

"What's that?" she asked, nodding toward it.

"I was going to leave you a coded message, in case you were late," Quinn said.

"What does it say?" Cody asked.

Quinn offered her a brochure about the Campanile. On the back were a series of letters that made no sense:

GVVX TFQXBSNQ SK XMLVN C&P — Z

Cody recognized the code as Caesar's cipher, and pulled out her decoder wheel from her backpack.

The letter after the dash at the end of the code—*Z*—
meant she was supposed to line up the outer letter
*A* with the inner wheel *Z* to decipher the message.
Then all she had to do was find each outer letter
and write down the corresponding inner letter.
She quickly began to decode the message, starting
with the outer letter *G*, which corresponded to the
inner letter *M*. Next came *V*, which meant *E*, and
so on, until she had finished.

*Code Buster's Key and Solution found on pp. 187, 192.*

Cody handed the brochure back to Quinn.

"I was going to tape it to the wall next to the
door, but now you're here . . . ," Quinn said, then he
unfolded the brochure. "This tells everything there
is to know about the Campanile. Ask me anything."

"Okay," Luke said. "What does *Campanile*
mean?"

"It's Italian for bell tower," Quinn said. "Guess
which bell tower is the most famous?"

"The Leaning Tower of Pisa," M.E. called out,

as if she were on a game show.

Quinn looked surprised. "Right."

Luke asked another question, reading from the brochure: "So what are carillons?"

"A bunch of bells," Quinn said, "connected to a keyboard, like a piano or organ. This one has been here long enough to hide those diamonds."

The Code Busters headed for the entrance to the Campanile. Luke pulled open the heavy glass door and held it for the others.

"Welcome to the Campanile," a young college student manning the tall desk said in greeting. He had black hair, covered by a blue and gold Cal Bears hat and matching jacket. "Here to take a tour?" he asked.

The kids nodded.

"Everyone under eighteen?"

*Duh*, Cody thought, but said yes, along with the others.

"Okay, it's a dollar per person."

The Code Busters handed over their money and listened to the introductory spiel as they waited for the elevator in the tiny lobby to arrive. After the car arrived and let out half a dozen passengers, the kids stepped in. They listened to another short lecture from the operator, a female student in jeans and a gray sweatshirt. She recited most of the information Quinn had already shared from the brochure, but added a few extra details about the tolling of the bells. "They ring on the hour, seven days a week, from eight in the morning till ten an night, and on the last day of class, at noon. Then the bells are silent until the end of finals."

That sounded foreboding to Cody. Finals must be tough at the university if they couldn't even play the bells.

The student continued reciting her memorized lines: "Although the tower is three hundred feet high you're going up two hundred feet to the observation deck. From there you'll be able to see the entire campus and all the way to San Francisco."

Luke raised his hand to ask a question, as if he were in school.

"Yes?" the student asked.

"I heard bones were kept in this tower. Is that true?"

The girl grinned as if Luke had said something funny. "I get that question a lot. As a matter of fact, yes, the paleontology department keeps fossils from the La Brea Tar Pits here because it's cool and dry and helps preserve them."

"Sweet. Can we see them?" Luke asked.

"I'm afraid not. Access to those floors requires a special key, and I don't have one. Sorry."

Luke pressed his lips together, looking disappointed, Cody thought. It would have been fun to see some old bones, but at the moment, they were on a different mission.

The elevator doors opened, and the kids stepped into a stairwell. Cody spotted a bronze plaque mentioned in the brochure, hanging on one of the walls.

"You may stay as long as you like," the girl said. "I come back every few minutes to pick people up and take them back down."

The Code Busters headed up the stairs and out onto the observation area that surrounded a small, enclosed room. The wind whipped through Cody, much like it had at the top of the lighthouse on Alcatraz. She zipped up her hoodie and pulled the hood over her head. Peering inside the tiny inner room, she saw a few of the massive steel bells, along with a row of horizontal bars that looked like giant organ pedals.

The kids had the place to themselves, so they could take their time and examine every accessible inch of the area. "You check that side, Cody," Quinn said, indicating the east side. "M.E., there." He pointed to the south side. "Luke, the west. I'll check out the north side."

The Code Busters spent several minutes exploring their assigned areas, searching for anything that might be a clue from one of Diamond Dave's gang—or even a diamond. After ten minutes or so of exploration, Quinn said, "I got nothing. You guys find anything?"

"Nope," Luke said. M.E. and Cody shook their heads.

Cody felt as if she would freeze to death if she stayed up in the tower much longer. Between her chattering teeth, she said, "Let me check one more place." She returned to the side of the tower that faced Alcatraz. "Anyone have a mirror?"

"Cody, this isn't really the time to check your face," Quinn said.

"It's not for that, Quinn. Wait, I have one! I almost forgot." Cody pulled out her iPhone and tapped on her mirror app. A picture of her face appeared, looking red and splotchy from the cold wind. She held the mirror out over the ledge and moved it around to see if she could spot anything on the outside.

"I think I see something!" Cody said, as she held the cell phone as steady as she could in her freezing hand. "Letters, and some numbers . . ."

The kids gathered around. "What does it say?" Quinn asked, straining to see the reflection in the phone mirror.

"I'll take a picture of it," she said, and clicked the phone's camera button. She pulled her hand in from the bitter cold and displayed the photograph she'd just snapped.

Sure enough, words and numbers had been carved underneath the ledge. She read them aloud: "'We ring, we chime, we toll: 9-18-36-3-2-12-17-5-16   10-17-16-2-18.'"

"That's from the plaque inside," Quinn said. "It's written in the brochure." He pulled the brochure from his pocket, opened it, and read the words: "'*We ring, we chime, we toll, Lend ye the silent part,*

*Some answer in the heart, Some echo in the soul.*'" He looked at the others with raised eyebrows.

"What about the numbers?" Cody asked. "That has to be some kind of code." She pulled out her notebook and wrote down the numbers, then tried to match them to letters in the alphabet. But the alphabet had only twenty-six letters. "It has something to do with the quote. Quinn, what's the ninth letter in the quote?"

"*C*," he said.

She wrote it down. "Okay, what's the eighteenth letter?"

"*L.*"

She continued counting off the numbers for Quinn to decipher. The thirty-sixth letter was *A*. The third letter was *R*. And so on. They looked at the word Cody had spelled out.

*Code Buster's Key and Solution found on pp. 188, 192.*

"Well," Quinn said, his face lighting up with recognition. "I guess that's where we're going next."

# Chapter 10

.E.'s eyes grew wide with excitement. "This
is so fun! A treasure hunt—for diamonds!"

"Look," Quinn said, heading for the other side of
the Campanile tower. "You can see it from here."
He pointed toward the foothills behind the campus,
where a white hotel was nestled. "See that big tower?"

This was the third tower on their treasure hunt,

Cody realized. This one belonged to the historic Claremont Hotel. Her mother had taken Cody there to celebrate her thirteenth birthday, and they'd had an afternoon tea party. The hotel had been built back in the early 1900s, and Cody had heard rumors that the hotel had been won in a checkers game by a miner—*and* was supposedly haunted.

But those weren't the only rumors associated with the hotel. Cody had also heard that the Claremont Hotel had a special fire escape—a spiral slide—so guests could get out quickly in case of an emergency. Years ago, kids from all over Berkeley would sneak into the hotel and ride the slide. But Cody's mom had told her that the hotel had destroyed that fire escape and replaced it with outdoor ladders.

"I'll bet there's something up there," Quinn said.

"Diamonds?" M.E. suggested.

Luke frowned. "I don't know, dude. Maybe

someone's just playing with us."

M.E. ignored him, clearly excited. "I heard it used to be a castle. I'd love to check it out."

Quinn typed something into his iPhone, then read. "Says here some old gold prospector struck it rich in the Mother Lode and built the place for his wife. She wanted it to look like an English castle. But when she died, he sold it and then it burned to the ground."

"How sad!" M.E. said.

Quinn continued reading. "That's when the guy won the property from the new owners and rebuilt it."

*So that rumor is true!* Cody thought. Hard to believe someone would gamble away his property.

"It also says sailors used to signal their loved ones who were staying at the hotel, using semaphore code. Look! It shows an example of a message that a guest received from her sea captain husband."

Quinn held up the message for everyone to see.

*Code Buster's Key and Solution found on pp. 188, 192.*

Cody recognized the flag code and translated each letter aloud.

"Cool," Luke said.

"Yeah, but does the article mention the spiral fire escape?" M.E. asked.

Quinn nodded. "But it was torn down in the seventies."

Luke frowned again. Cody knew he would have loved to go down that multistory slide.

"Listen to this," Quinn added. "Some kids started using the laundry chute as a slide instead."

Luke perked up. "Dude, that's awesome! Is it still there?"

"No. Says it's all boarded up. And get this. The hotel is supposed to be haunted!"

M.E.'s eyebrow shot up. Cody wished Quinn hadn't said anything about the place being haunted. She hadn't said anything because she knew M.E. would want to back out.

Quinn continued. "Says here the ghost of a young girl who died in the hotel haunts the fourth floor, and especially Room Four twenty-two. People who've stayed there say the TV turns on by itself and the chandelier lights flicker."

"That's just another legend," Luke said. "They probably made it up for the tourists."

"Maybe," Quinn said. "Anyway, the Claremont is right there if we take this shortcut. Let's go check it out."

"But we don't know where to go when we get there," M.E. said.

"We'll try the tower first," Quinn suggested. He took another look at the photo Cody had taken. "Hey, wait a minute. Did you guys see that?" He showed them the screen. "It looks like faint letters."

Before Cody could study the picture, a female student entered the glassed room in the center of the tower. Cody watched as she sat down on a bench, stretched and twisted her wrists, and then began to play the carillon. With her hands curled inward, she pressed on the large rectangular "keys" with the sides of her wrists.

Cody didn't recognize the tune, but the sound was deafening. All four of the Code Busters plugged their ears.'

Cody finger-spelled to the others,

*Code Buster's Key and Solution found on pp. 184, 192.*

They nodded and rushed down the stairwell to

the waiting elevator. By the time they reached the bottom of the tower, they were able to remove their fingers from their ears, but the bells were still loud. Once outside, Cody listened to the haunting sound of the ringing bells. It gave her goose bumps.

*It must take years to learn to play the carillon,* she thought, remembering the years she'd spent learning to play the family piano. But since Tana had been diagnosed with severe hearing loss, Cody had given up playing. It wasn't much fun since she couldn't share the songs with her deaf sister. In fact, no one in the family had played the instrument since then, not even her mother, who was a good pianist and could play just about any song by ear. Now the keyboard was closed up and the piano held a permanent display of knickknacks and photos.

Quinn pulled Cody from her sad memory. "Cody, let me see your phone again. I want to check that picture you took."

Cody handed her phone to Quinn. He studied the snapshot, then said, "These are letters!" With a flick of his fingers, he enlarged the screen so he could see the letters better, and read them aloud.

"E-T-U-H-C-Y-R-D-N-U-A-L."

"Read them again," M.E. said, pulling out her notebook.

Quinn repeated the string of letters.

"Et-uh-cyrd-nual?" M.E. asked, sounding out the letters like syllables.

"Sounds weird. Maybe it's someone's name," Luke offered. "Etuh Cyrdnual."

"That doesn't sound like a name," Quinn said. He squinted at it. "It's got to be some kind of code."

"Let me try," Luke said. He got out his own notebook and turned to the page with the reverse alphabet code. After trying to match the first few letters of the message with letters of the alphabet, he gave up. "That's not it."

"Maybe it's an anagram," Cody suggested.

130

Luke tried rearranging the letters to see if they'd spell any recognizable words. He came up with THE CRY LAND but had two *U*'s left over. He tried again and wrote LACY THUNDER with one left-over *U*. Finally, he wrote UNDER CUT HALY using all the letters, but that still didn't make sense.

M.E. tried it but only managed to come up with more nonsensical phrases like CHURN LATE DUY, DUEL YARN THUC, and CLUE RAD HUT NY.

Then Cody remembered using her mirror to see under the Campanile ledge, which gave her an idea. She took the notebook from M.E. and wrote the letters down in reverse.

L-A-U-N-D-R-Y-C-H-U-T-E

*Code Buster's Solution found on p. 192.*

"That's it!" Quinn said. "That's where we have to go when we get to the hotel!"

"Yeah," Luke said, "unless it's been destroyed, too, and we find another dead end."

Cody had stopped listening to the boys. She'd spotted a man in a black baseball cap standing only a few feet away reading a newspaper that covered his face. When he turned the page, Cody noticed he had a big black mustache and dark sunglasses. Then she noticed that his newspaper was upside down.

Whoever it was had been within hearing distance of the kids the whole time they'd been discussing the hunt for the diamonds.

Diamond Dave?

# Chapter 11

"uys," Cody whispered, "we'd better get out of
here. I think someone's watching us."

The three others glanced around.

"Don't look!" Cody said. "He'll see you! Be cool.
He's over by those bushes, pretending to read a
newspaper."

Quinn tried to look nonchalant as he surveyed

the area. M.E. put her head down and peeked around from under her bangs. Luke made no attempt to disguise his actions—he looked right in the direction Cody had indicated.

"Where?" Luke asked.

"Shhh! He'll hear you!" Cody sneaked another look.

The man was gone.

She blinked several times, as if clearing her eyes would make the man reappear. "I . . . I . . . He was just there. Standing, like, ten feet away. Reading a newspaper—upside down!" She searched the area but saw no sign of the man. "I know I saw someone."

"Whatever," Quinn said, shrugging. "Let's take the trail to the hotel. We'll keep an eye out to see if anyone follows us."

"What if he *is* following us?" M.E. asked. "And he tries to get us on the trail? Then what?"

Luke flexed his biceps. "I'll take care of him," he said.

Cody grinned.

"Meanwhile, let's run," Quinn said. "Ready? On the count of three: one . . . two . . . three!"

The Code Busters raced along the shortcut toward the hotel. The path was well worn, mostly uphill, and Cody kept glancing back to see if the man was following them. Maybe he wasn't spying on them. Maybe it had been her imagination.

The kids were puffing when they reached the grounds of the large white hotel. Cody scanned the plentiful tennis courts and two pools and wondered what it cost to stay there.

"Any sign of your mysterious stranger?" Quinn asked. He sounded as if he didn't believe her.

Cody shrugged and shook her head.

"Okay, let's see if we can find the laundry chute," Quinn said, excitement in his eyes.

The four kids entered the lobby of the grand hotel quietly, almost as if they were in church. Cody looked up at the high ceilings, then around at the

Victorian decor—ornate wallpaper, heavy chandeliers, velvety chairs, and the various antiques that filled the room.

"Now what?" M.E. whispered. "I don't think we can just go up to the front desk and ask where the laundry chutes are. They'll know we're up to something."

Cody nodded. "Let's get sodas at that café we passed. Maybe we can talk to the waiter to see if he knows anything about the chutes."

"Good idea," M.E. agreed. "I'm dying of thirst."

The kids headed over to the Paragon Restaurant, passing several fancy boutiques and shops along the way. The place was practically empty at that hour, with only a few couples at the bar. The kids found a table by the window, and Cody stared out at the view for a few moments, spotting Alcatraz looming under the Golden Gate Bridge. The waiter, an elderly man with thinning hair slicked back, wearing black pants and a black shirt, greeted them and handed each one a menu. His name tag read DELMAR MORRIS.

Cody blinked when she saw the prices. The price of food here was certainly higher than in the school cafeteria. After some discreet whispering and checking of funds, they decided on four lemonades and a basket of french fries to share.

The waiter appeared again at their table from seemingly nowhere, his arms straight down in front of him, his hands folded. Cody noticed a sparkling ring on his thin pinky finger. "Good afternoon, young people. What may I get you today?"

"Uh, we'd like four lemonades and some french fries, please," Quinn said.

The waiter nodded. "Very good. Anything else?"

"No, that's it." Quinn handed him the menus.

"Shall I put it on your room?"

The kids looked at each other, puzzled. Then Cody said, "No, thanks, we'll pay cash."

"Very good." He took the menus and disappeared.

"What did he mean, put it on your room?" M.E. asked.

"He meant we could charge it to our room at the hotel and pay for it later," Cody answered. "But we don't have a room."

Cody couldn't help checking the café entrance for any sign of the strange man she'd seen at the Campanile.

"Listen," Luke said, "this is it for me. If we don't find anything here, I say we give up. I've got a basketball game later today. Those diamonds were hidden a long time ago—there's no way they're still around. Either Diamond Dave got them back, or someone else found them . . . or they were never really there."

"Well, at least let's ask the waiter about the laundry chutes," Quinn said. "He looks like he's been around since the place was built. He should know where they are—if they still exist."

The waiter returned with a tray of four lemonades

in tall glasses and a plate of french fries sprinkled with bits of white and green things. He set the drinks at each place and put the fries in the middle, along with a bottle of ketchup.

"What's the green stuff?" Luke asked him.

"Just a little parsley, to give it color," the waiter said, standing at attention, his hands holding the empty tray in front of him. Cody noticed the sparkling ring again. It reminded her of her dad's class ring from the University of California. "These are our famous garlic fries. Will there be anything else?"

"Uh . . . yeah," Quinn said, looking up at him. "Have you been working here a long time?"

The waiter nodded. "More than fifty years. My father worked here as a maintenance man, and my son works here now as a tennis pro."

"That's cool," Luke said. "Do you live here, too?"

"No, I'm afraid not."

The waiter didn't seem to mind answering their

questions, nor did he seem to be in a hurry. No wonder—there were hardly any other customers in the café.

"We heard the hotel was haunted," M.E. said. Apparently, the thought of ghosts walking the halls was still on her mind.

"So I've heard," the waiter said. "But truthfully, I've never seen her."

"Her?" Cody asked.

"The little girl who supposedly haunts Room Four twenty-two. I think our guests like the idea of a haunted hotel—it reminds them of that movie *The Shining*. Still, I don't know how these rumors get started. Like ghosts, they never seem to die." He gave a crooked grin at his play on words, then he said, "So, no ghosts, but we've had everyone else here, from presidents to Hollywood stars. And now the four of you."

Cody felt herself blush. Did he really think they were staying at the hotel?

"About the rumors," Quinn continued. "We heard there were some fire escapes and laundry chutes that kids used to slide down. Are they still around?"

"Not anymore," the waiter said. "Both were dismantled some years ago. But you're right—local teenagers used to come up here and slide down the laundry chutes. I, myself, did at one time, when I was a lot younger, of course."

"Cool," Luke said, grinning. Cody could just picture Luke fearlessly sliding down the chutes.

"So they're really gone?" Quinn asked. His usually animated face was crestfallen.

"Yes. As you can imagine, they were a liability. If someone had gotten hurt, well, that wouldn't have been good. But there's still plenty of fun to be had here for young people. There are the pools, the gym, the spa, the tennis courts . . ."

*Still,* Cody thought, *nothing compares to a slide that travels from the top floor to the basement.*

*The basement . . .*

Before she could finish her thought, the waiter excused himself and left the kids to enjoy their drinks and fries. Quinn looked glum after learning the chutes no longer existed. This truly was a dead end, as Luke had predicted. The treasure hunt appeared to be over.

Suddenly, Cody noticed a figure in the café doorway. This man wore a long coat, a black baseball cap, glasses, and had a mustache. The only thing missing was the upside-down newspaper.

He'd followed them!

Cody pulled out her cell phone that she'd taken along, just in case. She began writing down numbers on a paper napkin, some with dots on one side or the other, some without.

"What are you doing?" M.E. asked as she watched Cody glance back and forth between her phone and the napkin.

"It's the telephone code," Quinn said, pulling

out his cell phone. "Each number stands for a let-ter on the phone keypad. If the letter is on the left, like *A*, you add a dot on the left— .2. If it's on the right, like *C*, you add a dot on the right, like 2., and if there's an extra letter, such as *WXYZ*, the two letters in the middle have no dots and you just have to figure out which one it is."

He touched the screen, revealing the phone key-pad, and started translating the code on his own napkin.

.9 3    .9 3 7 3    3. 6. 5. 5. 6. .9 3 .3 !

.6 .2 6    7. .8 .2 6 .3 4. 6 .4    4. 6    .3 6. 6. 7 .9 .2 9 !

*Code Buster's Key and Solution found on pp. 188, 193.*

After Quinn translated the code, the kids looked at the doorway.

The man had vanished.

"There's no man there," M.E. said.

"I swear I saw him," Cody said in a low voice.

"It was the same guy who was watching us at the Campanile. I saw him peeking in the doorway."

"There's no one there now," M.E. said.

"Are you sure you saw someone?" Quinn asked.

"I'm sure!" Cody said.

She looked at the others, waiting for them to believe her.

"Okay, I have an idea," Quinn said. "M.E. and I will take off and see if he follows us. If he does, we'll lead him on a wild-goose chase through the hotel. Luke and Cody, you act like you're going to stay here and finish your drinks, then head for the basement."

"Why the basement?" Luke asked, then stuffed a french fry in his mouth.

"That's where the laundry chute probably ended up," Quinn said. "Where they do all the hotel laundry. You guys take a look around, just to see if there's anything still there from the chute. We'll meet in the lobby in ten minutes. If the guy is still around—and following us—we'll tell the hotel detective."

"They have hotel detectives?" M.E. askcd.

Quinn nodded. He dug out money for his share of the bill, M.E. did the same, and the two Code Busters headed out of the café, trying to look suspicious by whispering and pretending to read a page of their codebook. Meanwhile, Luke and Cody tried to look casual, drinking their lemonade and finishing up the fries.

The waiter arrived with the bill, and Cody handed over the collected money.

"Thanks," Cody said, then added, "By the way, are guests allowed in the basement?"

The waiter shook his head. "No. That's for staff only." He paused a moment. "And those staff members use the service elevator, tucked into an alcove next to the guest elevators."

"Thanks," Cody said, smiling. She slid out of her chair. What a fun job the old waiter had, working in a place like this, with so much history and mystery and secret elevators and laundry chutes.

Cody saw no sign of the mysterious man as she and Luke left the café. Maybe he was tailing Quinn and M.E., as planned. Or maybe her imagination was working overtime. They headed for the service elevator, checking to make sure they weren't being followed, then ducked into the alcove and pushed the "Down" button. The doors opened and they stepped into the empty elevator car about the size of a hotel room. They rode to the bottom floor and stepped out into a dark hallway, lit by only a few bare bulbs. The air was stuffy, almost damp, and the sound of heavy-duty washing machines and dryers told them in which direction they'd find the laundry room. As they moved down the shadowy hall, they passed a few maids in uniforms speaking Spanish and stuffing bundles of bedding onto large rolling carts.

No one asked them what they were doing there.

Luke pointed to the laundry room. They entered an enormous space filled with washing machines and dryers, all running at once. Piles of sheets and blankets and comforters filled most of the floor, while freshly folded bedding was stacked on shelves. Several workers dressed in white uniforms monitored the machines.

An older woman folding sheets eyed them and frowned, but said nothing.

Cody gave her a friendly wave, hoping to charm her into accepting their presence.

The woman said something in Spanish that Cody didn't understand, then went back to her work.

Luke nudged Cody and pointed to a large hole in the side of one wall. They stepped over to inspect it and found the hole led upward—to blackness and a dead end. Cody got out her cell phone and used her flashlight app to light up the opening. Clearly, it had been blocked a few feet above with a piece of sheet metal.

Had this been the famous laundry chute?

If so, what did it have to do with the missing diamonds? Surely, the jewels hadn't been simply lying around in the laundry room all these years. Cody bent down and examined the edge of the chute. Scratches had been etched into the bottom of the opening. Cody noticed that they were in the shape of a circle.

It looked like a simple drawing made from vertical lines with dots on the tops of them. In the center of the circle of *i*'s was the number *422*.

Four twenty-two.

The number of the hotel room that was supposedly haunted by the young girl.

It had been carved inside a circle made of lines and dots.

Something was in that supposedly haunted room.

Cody *had* to find out what it was.

# Chapter 12

Ten minutes later, as planned, Cody and Luke met up with Quinn and M.E. in the lobby.

"How did it go?" Quinn asked. "Find anything?"

Cody glanced around to see if the strange man was lurking anywhere. No sign of him, but she couldn't shake the feeling that someone was lurking nearby. "Were you followed?" she asked.

"Nope," Quinn said. "I think you were imagining

things. Easy to do in a place like this."

Cody didn't respond, but she was certain she had seen the man earlier.

M.E. interrupted her thoughts. "We tried to go up to the hotel tower, but it's blocked. If there were diamonds up there, I doubt they're still around. But we couldn't get in to check for ourselves."

Quinn looked at Cody. "How about the basement?"

Cody pulled out her notebook and opened it to the page where she'd copied the drawing and number.

"What's that?" M.E. asked, peering at the page on tiptoe.

"Good question," Luke said. "That's what we'd like to know."

"The number!" Quinn said. "Four twenty-two. The same number as the haunted hotel room. Maybe there's something there."

"That's what I was thinking," Cody said. "But how are we supposed to get inside?"

"And do we really want to?" M.E. added, her eyebrows raised. "I mean, it could actually be haunted."

Luke rolled his eyes. "No worries, M.E., I won't let the ghost get you. But there's no way I can save you from your own imagination."

M.E. slapped him lightly on the arm. "Very funny."

"I have an idea," Quinn said. "Come on." He led the way to the elevators, this time the ones used by the guests, not the service elevator. The contrast between the two elevators impressed Cody. The service elevator car had bare steel walls and was large enough to fit a car inside, but the guest elevator was wood paneled, with a tile floor and posters of the many hotel offerings. Just as they stepped in, Cody thought she saw people step into the other elevator, including a man with a long coat, but he was turned away and other people were in the way. She couldn't be sure it was the same person who had been following them.

The elevator dinged on the fourth floor, and the kids stepped off. Cody paused for a second, waiting to see if the other elevator stopped on the fourth floor, too, but it bypassed their floor and continued up. The hallway was clear, except for a couple of maids' carts. Cody checked the signs that directed guests to their rooms, and pointed in the direction of the "400–425" wing. "That way," she said, after checking to see if anyone was nearby.

They moved slowly down the hallway and turned a corner. Cody thought she heard the elevator *ding*, signaling the arrival of a passenger, and paused again, but before she could check it out, Quinn stopped abruptly.

"Wait," he whispered.

"What?" M.E. asked.

"See those maids' carts?"

Temporarily forgetting her fears of being followed, Cody spotted the carts farther down the hall, where two women dressed in black-and-white maid uniforms were chatting.

"I'm going to pretend I forgot my key," Quinn said, "and ask them to let me in."

He started to head down the hall when M.E. grabbed his arm and yanked him back.

"What?" he asked, sounding irritated.

"Listen," she said. "What do you hear?"

He listened. "Nothing. Just the maids talking. Why?"

"And what are they saying?" M.E. asked.

"How should I know?" Quinn asked. "They're speaking Spanish."

"*Exactamente*," M.E. said. "Languages are just like codes, you know. And I happen to know this one. *Muévete*. Let me handle this."

"I can guess what *exactamente* means," Cody said. "Exactly. What does *muévete* mean?"

"Move!"

Cody grinned at her friend. M.E. was right—she was the only one who spoke Spanish. Cody knew only American Sign Language and codes. Someday she'd have to learn Spanish beyond *hola* and counting to ten.

M.E. took a deep breath and walked down the hall. The others pulled back around the corner so they wouldn't be spotted. If the maids saw them, they might think the four kids were up to something.

Cody pulled out her cell phone, tapped her Spanish-to-English dictionary app, and listened for M.E. to say a few words in Spanish. After a few moments, she heard, *"Disculpe. Perdí mis llaves. Por favor permítame entrar?"*

Cody looked up the words as fast as she could and guessed that M.E. had said something like: "Pardon me. I've lost my keys. Could you please let me in?"

*"Dónde están tus padres?"* the maid asked. ("Where are your parents?")

M.E. said something that Cody couldn't make out.

*"Cuál cuarto?"* the maid asked. (Which room?)

*"Cuatro dos dos,"* M.E. replied. Cody recognized the numbers. Four two two—the room number. After a few seconds, she heard M.E. say, *"Gracias."*

Had she really done it? Had she actually gotten the maids to open the door of the haunted room?

Moments later M.E. appeared from around the corner. "Come on!" she whispered. "After they opened the door, I left some paper stuck in the lock so we could get back inside. Hurry before they finish cleaning one of the other rooms. And be quiet!"

"You're brilliant!" Cody whispered, then tiptoed as she followed M.E. back to Room 422.

M.E. pulled the door open and waved the others inside. She closed the door gently, then let out a big sigh of relief.

"Your hands are shaking," Cody said.

"I know! I can't believe I just did that!" M.E. said, her cheeks rosy with excitement.

Quinn looked around. "Okay, we don't have

much time. The people staying in this room could come back any minute."

Cody scanned the room. The beds were made, but clothes were piled on top of the dresser drawers and strewn on chairs. "I don't think they have kids," she said, not spotting any toys or small outfits.

The kids looked at each other for a sign of what to do. Even though she didn't believe in ghosts, Cody felt a chill just being in the room that was supposedly haunted. But they had a job to do. "Let's get this over with and get out of here before we're caught," she said. "Look for something shaped like a circle, with . . . little sticks . . . and dots . . ."

They did a quick search of the bedroom and bathroom. The bedspread was a deep red velvet that matched the drapes, and the furniture was antique—nothing unusual. Cody sat on the bed and ran her fingers over the soft comforter. She lay back to gather her thoughts and looked up.

That's when she saw it.

A circle directly over her head, with, well . . . little sticks in it.

"The chandelier!" she said, sitting up and gazing at the overhead light. The dangling cherry-size crystals sparkled in the sunlight coming in through the open window. "See the little sticks? They look like candles, arranged in a circle." She got out the picture she'd drawn and compared it. "How many candles does the chandelier have?"

M.E. counted them aloud. "Thirteen!"

Cody counted the number of sticks on her drawing.

Thirteen.

She slipped off her shoes and stood on the bed to examine the chandelier. Each of the candle-shaped lights was topped with a large teardrop crystal, made to look like the candle's flame.

Suddenly, the door slammed open.

M.E. hadn't removed the paper wad from the lock.

"Hold it right there!" a deep voice boomed from the doorway.

M.E. screamed. They all spun around.

There stood the man Cody had described—long coat, black baseball cap, glasses, and a mustache. Somehow he *had* followed them—and they had not seen him!

In one hand the man held a mean-looking croquet mallet. "Get off that bed. Those diamonds are mine. And I appreciate you leading me right to them. I knew you kids were smart."

Cody jumped off the bed and moved against the wall, along with Quinn, Luke, and M.E. The man entered the room and closed the door behind him.

Grabbing at his face, he ripped the mustache from his upper lip, then removed the glasses and threw them to the floor. Instantly, Cody recognized him: it was Geoff, the guard from Alcatraz. The one who had let the Code Busters into the lighthouse. He must have heard their conversation at the lighthouse . . . and the Campanile . . . and in the lobby . . . and followed them!

He raised the mallet.

The kids recoiled against the wall.

He swung it—to Cody's surprise—not at the kids, but at the chandelier. The light fixture shattered, raining pieces of broken glass candles and sparkly gems onto the floor.

Geoff dropped the mallet and knelt down, scrambling for bits of the chandelier. While he ran his fingers through the debris, Cody had an idea. She slowly finger-spelled her plan to her friends, being careful not to attract the attention of the guard:

*Code Buster's Key and Solution found on pp. 184, 193.*

All three nodded—message received. She began inching her way toward the door, hoping the man was too distracted to notice.

He lifted up one of the crystals that had once

been a candle's "flame."

"I wanna thank you kids for helping me figure out where Diamond Dave's pals hid those stolen diamonds all those years ago. That's the only reason I've been working on the Rock, you know. I'd heard the stories, and I had a feeling they were true. And here they are." Geoff grinned, revealing his crooked, yellowed teeth. Cody wondered how anyone could look bad smiling, but this guy clearly did.

While the other Code Busters remained frozen to their spots against the wall, Cody moved closer to the door. Geoff continued to pick through the shattered chandelier parts and glass, collecting the crystal flames.

He held one up to the light coming in from the window. But instead of grinning again, his face tightened, and his smile turned to a grimace. Suddenly, he threw the crystals back onto the floor, then jumped up, spun around, and faced the kids, his face red with rage.

"Where are they?" he yelled.

In one quick movement, Cody snatched up the mallet Geoff had dropped on the floor and threw it at the angry man, hoping to hit him, or at least distract him. In the brief second it took him to dodge the mallet, she yanked the door open and ran.

"Oh, no, you don't!" Geoff the guard said. He lunged after her, grabbing hold of her hoodie.

Cody slipped out of the jacket and fled down the hall, screaming, "Help!"

The two maids appeared at the doors of the rooms they'd been cleaning.

One of the maids pushed her cart in front of the man as he tried to catch Cody. The other maid swung her mop at him, knocking him to the floor with a wet slap across the face, and smacked him again and again with the mop head. The maid with the cart pulled out her walkie-talkie and called, *"Seguridad!"*

Quinn, Luke, and M.E. appeared at the doorway,

quickly took in the situation, and ran to the guard. Luke grabbed one of the hotel sheets and threw it over the man as he lay on the floor holding his face. Meanwhile, Quinn shoved a cart up against him, blocking him against the wall.

M.E. just screamed.

Moments later two security guards stormed in from the stairwell.

# Chapter 13

The police—including Officer Jones, Cody's mother—arrived moments after the two security guards had cuffed Geoff. The maids were talking to an officer who knew Spanish, while a few hotel guests gathered behind a police line, hoping to see what all the commotion was about. Cody and the other kids stood by and watched as two officers took the handcuffed man away. As Geoff passed by Cody, he glared at her, sending a cold chill down her spine.

Cody's mother approached the kids, who were huddled together, watching the scene.

"Ooookay," she said, hands on her hips and standing at attention in her uniform. "You want to tell me what happened here?"

Cody looked at the others, hoping they'd step up and explain the situation, but they remained mute and stared at the floor. Cody took a deep breath. "We were . . ."

Cody's dad suddenly appeared from down the hall. "Dakota! What happened? What are you doing here? I thought you were at the Berkeley campus working on a school project."

"I was just asking her the same thing," Cody's mom said to him.

"Dad, what are you doing here?" Cody asked, repeating her dad's question.

"Your mother called me. What's going on?"

"I'm trying to tell you," Cody said, feeling frustrated at the interrogation. "We were looking for . . . diamonds."

"What?" her dad asked, his face a picture of disbelief.

"It's a long story, Dad," Cody began to explain. "It started the day before our trip to Alcatraz. I got this strange e-mail message. It was a poem that hinted about there being some kind of treasure on the island. So when we went on our field trip the next day, we looked for clues."

Mr. Jones seemed to go pale. He slapped his hand on his forehead. "Oh, no . . . I didn't mean . . ."

Cody squinted at him. "Dad? What's wrong?"

He looked at Cody's mom, then glanced at the four kids. "I'm the one who sent that e-mail message. Since you kids love secret codes and messages so much, I thought it would be fun to send you on a sort of treasure hunt around the prison island. But you were never meant to end up here."

Officer Jones glared at her ex-husband. But before she could speak, Cody asked, "You wrote that poem? You sent us looking for those seats? And inside the lighthouse?"

Mr. Jones nodded until she asked the last question. "Inside?" he asked. "No. The clue was on the *outside*. It was supposed to lead you to another clue, and that clue was to lead you to the exercise yard, then the gardens, and then the gift shop. The last code said, 'Surprise! Love, your dad.' I hid it under a book about Alcatraz in the shop."

Cody frowned, remembering the note about ringing a bell—and that she hadn't had a chance to read the rest of the message before the guard snatched it out of her hands. She glanced at her friends.

"I didn't see that note until we were leaving the lighthouse, and then I forgot about it because we assumed it had something to do with the Campanile bell tower. When we first came to the lighthouse, the door was open, so the note was hidden. The guard said we could go inside if we were quick—so we climbed up to the top. We found a message carved into the wall that gave us directions to the Campanile. He must have overheard us talking about finding the diamonds during the tour—and again in the lighthouse—and followed us to the campus, then here. I thought it might have been Matt the Brat or even Diamond Dave following us, but it was the guard. He thought we would lead him to Diamond Dave's stash."

"Cody, you told me you needed to go to the campus to work on a class project."

Quinn spoke up. "It was a project, just not a *class* project. Then when we got another clue at the Campanile tower, we wanted to follow it."

"Another clue?" Mr. Jones asked.

"Yeah, the one that sent us here, to the Claremont," Luke said.

"But that guard followed us," M.E. added,

nervously twisting her long hair into a spiral.

"So who is Diamond Dave?" Cody's mom asked.

Her dad spoke up. "The ranger told the kids a story about Diamond Dave on the tour. I'd read about him online—that's where I got the idea for a treasure hunt. But I had no idea it would lead them here. With a maniac following them." Her dad suddenly looked tired. Cody knew that look: extreme worry. No wonder. She'd given her dad— and her mom—quite a scare.

"I'm sorry, Mom, Dad," Cody said. "We thought we were just following clues to an old mystery. We figured if the diamonds were still there, it would be cool to find them."

"And maybe buy some new night-vision goggles or a high-tech GPS for our club," Quinn added.

"All right," Officer Jones said. "I'm sure I'm going to have more questions for you later, but for now, I want you to go down to the restaurant and wait for me there while we finish up here. I'll give you guys some money. Buy yourselves something to eat. And stay there!"

"I'll go with them," Mr. Jones said.

Cody's mom nodded her thanks.

The kids headed for the elevator in silence and rode the car down to the lobby level with Mr. Jones, who kept glancing from one Code Buster to another, saying nothing. When they reached the café, the kids returned to the table they'd occupied earlier, and Cody's dad pulled up an extra seat. She glanced out at Alcatraz, where all of this mess had really started.

"Dad—"

"Mr. Jones—"

"Kids—"

Everyone spoke at once. The kids stopped talking; Cody's dad continued. "Look, guys. This is partly my fault. I shouldn't have made up that treasure hunt. I had no idea you'd miss my clue and find clues to a treasure hunt more than fifty years old! But next time, let us know where you're going. You were lucky this time."

The Code Busters nodded.

The same waiter who had waited on them earlier—Delmar Morris—appeared and stood at attention, once again holding his hands together in front of him. Cody noticed the ring again and wondered if it was a university class ring, like her dad's.

"So, you're back for more lemonade and french fries," the waiter said, a small smile playing at his lips. "And you've brought a guest?"

"This is my dad," Cody said glumly.

"A pleasure to meet you, sir. What can I get for you all this time? Another round?"

"How about lunch?" Mr. Jones asked the others.

They nodded vigorously; they were all very hungry after having only a few fries and a drink earlier.

"How about five cheeseburgers," Mr. Jones suggested to the kids. They nodded.

The waiter bowed slightly, then asked, "Did you

find the laundry chute?"

Cody shook her head. "You were right. They're gone, except for an opening in the wall that's been sealed up."

"But we found a message there," Quinn spoke up.

"Really?" the waiter asked. "A message?"

"Yeah," Luke said. "There was a drawing and the number four twenty-two—the same number as the haunted hotel room. When we got to the room, we realized that the drawing was of the chandelier in that room. We thought maybe there were diamonds hidden in there . . ." Luke trailed off.

"Ah, the diamonds," the waiter mused. "You're referring to that story I heard as a kid. When my father was the maintenance man back then, there was a fellow who insisted on staying in the haunted room—Room Four twenty-two—and paid quite a lot extra for it, I understand. The next day, my father was sent to the room to replace the chandelier. When he arrived, he found the fixture had been completely removed from the ceiling and had vanished, along with the mysterious fellow. He had to install a new one—not half as nice as the original. And he didn't like being in that room. The ghost rumors, you know."

"Did he see the ghost of the little girl?" M.E. asked.

"No—at least, he never mentioned it."

"What about the diamonds?" Luke asked.

"He didn't see any diamonds, but he found a crystal from the old chandelier, buried in the carpet. He had it made into a ring as a memento of the biggest theft ever to occur at the Claremont." The waiter held up his hand. "He gave it to me before he died. I plan to give it to my son someday."

Cody blinked when she saw the ring. The crystal in the middle of the bronze setting sparkled in the light. Could it be . . . ?

"Well, if you'll excuse me, I'll get those cheeseburgers going." The waiter hurried off.

Cody looked at the others. "Guys!" she whispered. "Did you see that ring on his pinkie finger?"

"Yeah, what of it?" Quinn asked.

Luke turned to Cody. "You don't think . . ."

M.E.'s eyes brightened. "Do you think it could be?"

Cody's dad held his hands up. "Whoa. Wait a minute. What are you kids talking about?"

"His ring!" Cody said. "What if it's not a crystal, but a real diamond that was hidden in the old chandelier?"

The waiter returned with their drinks. As he set them in front of each place, the kids couldn't take their eyes off his ring. After he placed the last drink on the table, Mr. Jones leaned over to read the older man's name tag, then said, "Excuse me, Mr. Morris, have you ever had that ring appraised?"

The waiter chuckled. "Oh, no. It just has sentimental value, from my dad. I'm sure it has no monetary value."

Mr. Jones met the waiter's eyes. "I highly recommend that you do."

The waiter's eyes fluttered as he looked down at his ring. He cocked his head, smiled, and left the table.

Cody grinned at her dad. Something good might come out of this after all.

A few days later, Mr. Jones arrived unexpectedly at Cody's mother's house. The Code Busters were studying in Cody's room when he entered. Quinn was on the floor, working on a math paper. Luke sat in the beanbag chair, reading a skateboarding magazine. M.E. was at the computer, and Cody lay on her stomach on her bed, looking over her spelling words.

"Hi, Dad!" Cody said. "What are you doing here?"

"Hey, can't a dad come see his daughter and her code-busting friends when he wants to?" he asked.

"Uh . . . sure, I guess. So what's up?"

Mr. Jones sat on the edge of her bed.

"I got a call," he said.

*Uh-oh*, Cody thought. More fallout from their misadventure over the weekend. She tensed up, waiting for the bad news, certain her mother would ground her until she turned eighteen. "Yeah? From who?" she asked. "The hotel said they weren't going to press charges against us, and they were actually glad that their security guards and maids had helped to capture Geoff."

"No, not from the hotel, exactly. From the waiter, Mr. Morris."

Cody sat up. "What did he want?"

"He had the ring appraised yesterday."

Cody shivered with excitement. "Really?"

"You were right. The crystal turned out to be a diamond. And it's apparently worth quite a lot of money."

"You're kidding!" Cody squealed. The other Code Busters high-fived at the news.

"And he wants to do something for the Code Busters, to thank you all."

"For real?" Quinn said.

"Yes. He's invited you all to a day of swimming at the Claremont and lunch at the Bayview Café. All the burgers and fries you can eat. And this will make you smile—he's throwing in some tech equipment for the club."

"Awesome!" Luke said.

"Sweet!" M.E. nearly shouted.

"How did he know where to find us?" Cody asked. "He must be a pretty good detective."

"He remembered my name from my credit card, called me, and told me the news."

Cody felt extremely satisfied with the results of their treasure hunt. "See, Dad? Being a Code Buster pays off."

Mr. Jones patted her leg and stood up.

"Yeah, well, remember: snooping around in other people's business can also get you into trouble. So enjoy your code busting, but don't get carried away, hear?"

"Sure, Dad," Cody said.

"Oh, and this must've fallen out of your backpack for you." He handed her a large manila envelope. "Your mom said to bring it up to you. See you guys later." He left the kids to their studies, closing the door behind him.

Cody studied the envelope addressed to "The Code Busters." There was no return address. She opened it and found a sheet of paper inside. There appeared to be nothing written on either side. At the bottom of the envelope, Cody spotted a pen.

She held it up.

"What is it?" M.E. asked.

"I'm not sure," Cody answered. She uncapped the pen, then began swiping it across one side of the paper. Letters were revealed.

"It's an invisible ink decoder!" Quinn said. "Cool! It looks like someone wrote a message on the paper in invisible ink, and included the decoder pen! What does it say?"

Cody continued to color the paper with the pen, until all the letters were revealed. She held it up for the others to see.

"It makes no sense," Luke said, looking at the ten-by-ten-square grid filled with random letters.

| C | P | I | R | A | T | E | S | A | M |
|---|---|---|---|---|---|---|---|---|---|
| A | B | C | D | E | F | G | E | H | I |
| R | I | J | V | K | L | M | A | N | S |
| M | O | P | I | W | H | E | R | E | S |
| E | Q | R | S | S | T | U | C | V | I |
| L | W | X | I | Y | Z | A | H | B | O |
| W | A | N | T | S | C | D | E | E | N |
| H | F | F | G | H | I | J | D | K | L |
| O | O | M | N | T | H | E | O | P | Q |
| T | R | E | A | S | U | R | E | R | S |

He was right, Cody thought. It didn't make sense—yet. But four of the words jumped out at her immediately—the ones along the edges of the puzzle. She recognized it as a hidden-word puzzle. Inside the grid were strings of letters—going vertically, horizontally, and diagonally—that formed familiar words. Together the kids went to work on the puzzle, circling the words as they found them. Soon they had a list of random words.

CARMEL

PIRATES

MISSION

TREASURE

WHERE

WANTS

THE

TO

VISIT

SEARCHED

FOR

WHO

Cody noticed the leftover letters were in alphabetical order.

"This is like an anagram of words," M.E. said.

Cody began rearranging the words on a sheet
of paper. It didn't take her long to put the words
together so they made sense.

*Code Buster's Solution found on p. 193.*

"It sounds like we're going on another field trip
soon," she exclaimed! "I'll bet it's from Ms. Stad."

"Cool!" Luke said. "I love pirates. This should
be fun."

Cody looked at Luke. "Do you really think
there's a hidden treasure?"

Luke shrugged. "I guess we'll find out soon
enough!"

# CODE BUSTER'S

# Key Book
# &
# Solutions

## Finger Spelling:

a b c d e f g h

i j k l m n o p q r

s t u v w x y z

1 2 3 4 5 6 7 8 9

## Pig Latin:

To speak pig Latin, take the first consonant of the word, add *ay* to it, and move it to the end of the word. For example, to say "Cody" in pig Latin, you would say "ody" first, then "Cay," to form "ody-cay." If the word is only one syllable, like "Quinn," use the first letter (or two) to form the end of the word, such as "inn-quay."

## Cryptogram Key:

| A | B | C | D | E | F | G | H | I | J | K | L | M |
|---|---|---|---|---|---|---|---|---|---|---|---|---|
| T | H | E | R | O | C | K | A | L | I | B | Q | F |

| N | O | P | Q | R | S | T | U | V | W | X | Y | Z |
|---|---|---|---|---|---|---|---|---|---|---|---|---|
| Z | G | J | M | P | N | D | V | S | Y | U | X | W |

## Alphanumeric Code (1):

| 1 | 2 | 3 | 4 | 5 | 6 | 7 | 8 | 9 | 10 | 11 | 12 | 13 | 14 | 15 |
|---|---|---|---|---|---|---|---|---|----|----|----|----|----|----|
| A | B | C | D | E | F | G | H | I | J | K | L | M | N | O |

| 16 | 17 | 18 | 19 | 20 | 21 | 22 | 23 | 24 | 25 | 26 |
|----|----|----|----|----|----|----|----|----|----|----|
| P | Q | R | S | T | U | V | W | X | Y | Z |

## Tap Code:

|   | 1 | 2 | 3 | 4 | 5 |
|---|---|---|---|---|---|
| 1 | A | B | C | D | E |
| 2 | F | G | H | I | J |
| 3 | L | M | N | O | P |
| 4 | Q | R | S | T | U |
| 5 | V | W | X | Y | Z |

185

## LEET Code:

| | | |
|---|---|---|
| A = 4 | J = _\| | S = $ |
| B = 8 | K = \|< | T = + |
| C = ( | L = \|_ | U = (_) |
| D = \|) | M = /\/\ | V = \/ |
| E = 3 | N = /\/ | W = \/\/ |
| F = \|= | O = () | X = * |
| G = 6 | P = \|* | Y = \\\|/ |
| H = # | Q = (,) | Z = 2 |
| I = ! | R = \|2 | |

## Morse Code:

| | | | |
|---|---|---|---|
| A .- | H .... | O --- | V ...- |
| B -... | I .. | P .--. | W .-- |
| C -.-. | J .--- | Q --.- | X -..- |
| D -.. | K -.- | R .-. | Y -.-- |
| E . | L .-.. | S ... | Z --.. |
| F ..-. | M -- | T - | |
| G --. | N -. | U ..- | |

Phonetic Alphabet:

| | | |
|---|---|---|
| A = Alpha | J = Juliet | S = Sierra |
| B = Bravo | K = Kilo | T = Tango |
| C = Charlie | L = Lima | U = Uniform |
| D = Delta | M = Mike | V = Victor |
| E = Echo | N = November | W = Whisker |
| F = Foxtrot | O = Oscar | X = X-ray |
| G = Golf | P = Papa | Y = Yankee |
| H = Hotel | Q = Quebec | Z = Zulu |
| I = India | R = Romeo | |

Caesar's Cipher:

| ABCD | EFGH | I J K L | MNOP | QRST | UVWXYZ |
|---|---|---|---|---|---|
| Z A L V | DPMJ | XFNW | ORBK | SCIU | QEHTGY |

## Alphanumeric Code (2):

1 2　3 4 5 6,　　7 8　　9 10 11 12 13,　　14 15　　16 17 18 19,

**We  r i n g,  we   c h i m e,   we   t o l l,**

20 21 22 23　　24 25　　26 27 28　　29 30 31 32 33 34　　35 36 37 38…

**L e n d   y e   t h e   s i l e n t   p a r t…**

## Semaphores:

a　b　c　d　e　f　g　h　i

j　k　l　m　n　o　p　q　r

s　t　u　v　w　x　y　z

## Telephone Code:

| | | | | |
|---|---|---|---|---|
| A = .2 | B = 2 | C = 2. | D = .3 | E = 3 |
| F = 3. | G = .4 | H = 4 | I = 4. | J = .5 |
| K = 5 | L = 5. | M = .6 | N = 6 | O = 6. |
| P = .7 | Q/R = 7 | S = 7. | T = .8 | U = 8 |
| V = 8. | W = .9 | X/Y = 9 | Z = 9. | |

# Chapter 1

*Sudoku:*

| 5 | 7 | 9 | 1 | 6 | 3 | 8 | 2 | 4 |
|---|---|---|---|---|---|---|---|---|
| 8 | 4 | 3 | 2 | 9 | 7 | 5 | 6 | 1 |
| 2 | 1 | 6 | 5 | 8 | 4 | 3 | 9 | 7 |
| 4 | 6 | 8 | 9 | 2 | 5 | 7 | 1 | 3 |
| 1 | 2 | 7 | 6 | 3 | 8 | 9 | 4 | 5 |
| 3 | 9 | 5 | 7 | 4 | 1 | 2 | 8 | 6 |
| 6 | 3 | 4 | 8 | 7 | 2 | 1 | 5 | 9 |
| 9 | 8 | 1 | 3 | 5 | 6 | 4 | 7 | 2 |
| 7 | 5 | 2 | 4 | 1 | 9 | 6 | 3 | 8 |

*Anagrams:* **house, school, monkey, danger (or garden) , finger (or fringe), forgot, spelling, scream**

*Pig Latin:* **My parents do, too!**

*Cody's e-mail message:*

**I dare you to visit the haunted lighthouse on Alcatraz**

*Finger spelling:* **Mom says it's time to go home.**

## Chapter 2

*Wacky Word:* **Locked up in jail**

*Finger spelling:* **Have fun at school.**

## Chapter 3

*Cryptogram:* **1. Al Capone  2. Machine Gun Kelly**

**3. Creepy Carpis  4. Birdman  5. Doc Barker**

**6. Pretty Boy Floyd**

**Pretty Boy Floyd was never at Alcatraz**

## Chapter 4

*Alphanumeric code (1):* **1. FIVE feet by NINE feet.**

**2. SINK, COT, and TOILET.**

**3. 336, and 6 SOLITARY.**

**4. YES, ONE PER MONTH.**

**5. TOO EXPENSIVE and RUN DOWN.**

**6. PRISONERS COULDN'T TALK,**

   **so they used a TAPPING CODE.**

**7. 36 TRIED, but NONE WERE SUCCESSFUL.**

**8. YES. They were BUILT BY SOLDIERS.**

*Tap code:*

**W    A    T    E    R**

**C    O    O    L**


Chapter 5

*LEET code:* **CANDLE ON THE WATER**

*Morse code:* **What do we do now?**


Chapter 6

*Morse code:* **S  O  S  =  Save  Our  Ship  =  Help!**

*Riddle:* **It's a lighthouse!**

*Finger spelling:* **LIGHTHOUSE**


Chapter 7

*Phonetic alphabet:* **Ship in distress.**

*Morse code:* **Campanile bell tower 110 degrees.**


Chapter 8

*ABC code:* **Does this clue ring a bell?**

*Zigzag code:*

**M e a t e a p n l t m r o a t n**

**e t t h c m a i e o o r w t e**

**Meet at the Campanile tomorrow at ten.**


Chapter 9

*Caesar's cipher:*

**MEET UPSTAIRS IN TOWER L & K**

*Alphanumeric code (2):* **Claremont Hotel**


Chapter 10

*Semaphore code:* **Constance - arriving tomorrow noon - Edward.**

*Finger spelling:* **Let's go.**

*Mirror code:* E-T-U-H-C-Y-R-D-N-U-A-L

**LAUNDRY CHUTE**

## Chapter 11

*Telephone code:* **We were followed! Man standing in doorway!**

## Chapter 12

*Finger spelling:* **I'll make a run for it.**

## Chapter 13

*Hidden Word Search Puzzle:*

| C | P | I | R | A | T | E | S | A | M |
|---|---|---|---|---|---|---|---|---|---|
| A | B | C | D | E | F | G | E | H | I |
| R | I | J | V | K | L | M | A | N | S |
| M | O | P | I | W | H | E | R | E | S |
| E | Q | R | S | S | T | U | C | V | I |
| L | W | X | I | Y | Z | A | H | B | O |
| W | A | N | T | S | C | D | E | E | N |
| H | F | F | G | H | I | J | D | K | L |
| O | O | M | N | T | H | E | O | P | Q |
| T | R | E | A | S | U | R | E | R | S |

**WHO WANTS TO VISIT THE CARMEL MISSION WHERE PIRATES SEARCHED FOR TREASURE?**

Finger spelling:

Chapter Title Translations

**Chapter 1** *The Shadow Knows*

**Chapter 2** *The Torn Message*

**Chapter 3** *More Pieces to the Puzzle*

**Chapter 4** *The Search for Two Seats*

**Chapter 5** *To Be or Not to Be?*

**Chapter 6** *The Haunted Lighthouse*

**Chapter 7** *No Admittance—Keep Out!*

**Chapter 8** *The Zigzag Puzzle*

**Chapter 9** *Carillon at Campanile*

**Chapter 10** *The Haunted Hotel*

**Chapter 11** *Someone Is Watching*

**Chapter 12** *Room 422*

**Chapter 13** *Diamond in the Rough*

*For more adventures with the Code Busters Club, go to www.CodeBustersClub.com.*

There you'll find:

1. Full dossiers for Cody, Quinn, Luke, and M.E.
2. Their blogs
3. More codes
4. More coded messages to solve
5. Clues to the next book
6. A map of the Code Busters neighborhood, school, and mystery
7. A contest to win your name in the next Code Busters book.

# Suggestions for How Teachers Can Use the Code Busters Club Series in the Classroom

Kids love codes. They will want to "solve" the codes in this novel before looking up the solutions. This means they will be practicing skills that are necessary to their class work in several courses, but in a non-pressured way.

The codes in this book vary in level of difficulty so there is something for students of every ability. The codes move from a simple code wheel—Caesar's Cipher wheel—to more widely accepted "code" languages such as Morse code, semaphore and Braille.

In a mathematics classroom, the codes in this book can easily be used as motivational devices to teach problem-solving and reasoning skills. Both of these have become important elements in the curriculum at all grade levels. The emphasis throughout the book on regarding codes as *patterns* gives students a great deal of practice in one of the primary strategies of problem solving. The strategy of "Looking for a Pattern" is basic to much of mathematics. The resolving of codes demonstrates how important patterns are. These codes can lead to discussions of the logic behind why they "work," (problem solving). The teacher can then have the students create their own codes (problem formulation) and try sending secret messages to one another, while other students try to "break the code." Developing and resolving these new codes will require a great deal of careful reasoning on the part of the students. The class might also wish to do some practical research in statistics, to determine which letters occur most frequently in the English language. (*E*, *T*, *A*, *O*, and *N* are the first five most widely used letters and should appear most often in coded messages.)

This book may also be used in other classroom areas of study such as social studies, with its references to code-breaking machines, American Sign Language, and Braille. This book raises questions such as, "Why would semaphore be important today? Where is it still used?"

In the English classroom, spelling is approached as a "deciphering code." The teacher may also suggest the students do some outside reading. They might read a biography of Samuel Morse or Louis Braille, or even the Sherlock Holmes mystery "The Adventure of the Dancing Men."

This book also refers to modern texting on cell phones and computers as a form of code. Students could explain what the various "code" abbreviations they use mean today and why they are used.     *—Dr. Stephen Krulik*

*Dr. Stephen Krulik has a distinguished career as a professor of mathematics education. Professor emeritus at Temple University, he received the 2011 Lifetime Achievement Award from the National Council of Teachers of Mathematics.*